Dame Durden's Daughter

Dame Durden's Daughter

Joan Smith

ISIS
LARGE PRINT
Oxford

Copyright © Joan Smith, 1978

First published in Great Britain 2005
by
Robert Hale Limited

Published in Large Print 2009 by ISIS Publishing Ltd.,
7 Centremead, Osney Mead, Oxford OX2 0ES
by arrangement with
Robert Hale Limited

British Library Cataloguing in Publication Data
Smith, Joan, 1938–
    Dame Durden's daughter.
    1. Great Britain - - History - - George III,
    1760–1820 - - Fiction.
    2. Love stories.
    3. Large type books.
    I. Title
    813.5'4–dc22

ISBN 978–0–7531–8480–6 (hb)
ISBN 978–0–7531–8481–3 (pb)

Printed and bound in Great Britain by
T. J. International Ltd., Padstow, Cornwall

CHAPTER
ONE

How the Duke of Saymore and his sanctimonious spouse had come to sire a demon was a subject of frequent and regretful discourse between them, but that such a disgrace had been visited on them was known to the whole kingdom. Their only son — such a sweet babe he had been, too — was hero of a thousand scandals before he reached his majority and another couple of thousand since that day. He had broken a score of bones while still in breeches by riding the wildest nags in the county, had driven two tutors to drink with his escapades and one to the local roundhouse for aiding him in kidnapping a local beauty. He had also announced himself publicly as a supporter of Napoleon Bonaparte, and his father a Tory! It was assumed as a matter of course that the child of every unwed mother in Saymore's domain was to be laid at his door; that the staggering sums paid out by his papa went to either the moneylenders or the muslin company; and that he would never get into Oxford, thus breaking a long family tradition. In the earliest family records, the first Duke of Saymore had gone to Oxford in the twelfth century, and every Duke of Saymore since had done likewise. It was perhaps this

1

long history that opened the portals of the place to the upcoming Duke, but his stay there was brief. Before the first term was out, he was sent down for striking a master.

His mama prayed for him, and with him when he was home, three times a day. He was made to memorize the first ten chapters of Deuteronomy and was led to church every Sunday, where he placed tacks on the seats and freed mice, frogs or any other animals of a size to slip into his pockets. With all this religion, how did it come he remained possessed of Satan? His aunt Sara declared it was a judgement on the parents for not entering the strict Methodist religion as she had done herself in a bid to reclaim him; and in desperation the Duchess tried even this extreme measure for six months, but to no avail. Helver remained the wayward youth he had always been and when at sixteen he sold his prize stallion to buy the Widow Malone a garish set of garnets made up in exact duplicate of the Saymore rubies, the ladies reverted to their comfortable Episcopalian faith and gave up hope of his ever amounting to a hill of beans.

And not another son to comfort the parents, or even a daughter. Just this one child of their old age. This was deeply regretted until it occurred to the Duchess that all their offspring might have been tainted, and she became resigned to the great wisdom of the Almighty. She searched the family records for a preview of this streak of evil that must have lain dormant in her blood or the Saymores' all these generations but found nothing. Bishops, magistrates, cabinet ministers, one

Prime Minister and one Lord Mayor of London were the ancestors that had led to this unsavoury culmination. There was no explaining it. The devil had got a toehold on the family tree, and the best and likeliest thing to happen was for this last twig to die before producing a legitimate heir.

They were always happy to ship him off to any unsuspecting relative for a few months, and he happy to go; but he invariably came home with some new disgrace dogging his steps — a son led astray, a good match in the family ruptured (best not to inquire too minutely as to the how or why), or, at the very least, the neighbourhood in an uproar. Helver reached twenty-three with very few signs of improvement, and the despondent parents were half relieved when he expressed a desire to go to Europe to view the Congress of Vienna. It would give England a little respite from him.

Perhaps the Saymores exaggerated their son's notoriety. He was not discussed every day in the drawing rooms of London, as they imagined him to be; but in the Duke's village he was certainly the topic of paramount discussion, and Tisbury was the real center of their world. It was a sleepy little place in the south of Wiltshire where things had not changed greatly in a hundred years except for the enclosure of the common lands. The neighbouring roads were lately improved; but a visit to Bath twenty-five miles north was still a major trip not taken by many and London, a hundred miles away to the east, was a fabled spot peopled with characters only half believed in. The real king and queen were the Duke and Duchess and their son, Helver Trebourne, who was never called Lord Helver or given any sort of a title, was the heir-apparent to the throne. His frolics were more known and talked about in the village than those of the other prince, and also taken more seriously. Prinney might have his closet wife and his public wife, but Mrs Fitzherbert and Princess Caroline were not personally known to them, whereas Helver's women were their own neighbours, cousins, and daughters. No wonder if they should find the Widow Malone, who jostled elbows with them at the butcher in silk gowns and garnets, a more fascinating creature than a famous lady in London. Helver was a prime one, called Helver by them all, down to the lowliest dustman, despite his high position. He had roamed free amongst them from his earliest years, cadging sweets and chasing dogs when he was young, and their daughters when he was a little older. As he was not home to ascend the throne when his father died, he went on being "that Helver Trebourne" in their minds and talk, and was not officially given his title.

No tutor could handle Helver for a whole day. With a mind like quicksilver, he finished the day's prepared lessons in a morning and in desperation they gave him the afternoon off. He read and he thought, and what he thought was that the world was unfair. Why should so few have so much, and so many be so poor? Why should he, who had never done a day's work in his life, live in a palace while Joe Styles, with ten children, worked like a dog and lived in a two-room hovel? Still he liked his palace very much, and was not such a

4

philosopher that he ever envisaged moving Joe and his brood into the Hall, but he thought about such things. He championed the French Revolution when he was taught it and did not share the national hatred of Frenchies. He thought they had a good deal of gumption to take a stand and rather wished he had been born a French commoner twenty years sooner than he had been born an English nobleman. He began calling himself a Republican when he was seventeen and bought a white hat to proclaim his status, but failed to excite his elders with it as they did not realize its significance. He had been a dandy a month before, and they thought it only the newest fad from London.

All things considered, the Saymores thought they could part with their son for a few months if he wanted to go to Vienna. He was bound to embroil himself in the lowest forms of debauchery while there, but at least he wouldn't be doing it in England. In November of 1814 he left the Hall. That he never returned would be better luck than his mama could hope for, though after a time she did fall to wondering what had happened to him. She assumed this rest from her son's presence would have a beneficial influence on her husband's failing health, but it proved to be not the case. Helver was not gone a month before the Duke was struck down with an ague and taken to his Maker, there presumably to render an account of himself and this monster he had produced.

While Helver Trebourne frolicked amidst the lively international set gathered to make merry in Vienna, breaking ladies' hearts and men's heads, his father was laid to rest in the family plot. Helver had not been in Vienna long before he heard of plans by various groups to go to Elba and meet the lately deposed Emperor. Without a moment's hesitation he turned his back on the Congress and headed south, to be one of the first to be presented to Napoleon. He liked him amazingly and went on to Corsica to see his place of birth. With only the Mediterranean Sea between Corsica and Spain, it seemed foolish not to go on and have a look while he was so close. Portugal, situated between Spain and the Atlantic, was taken in along the way, and with a run of luck at the gaming tables he was enabled to spend some considerable months in these latter two countries. His mama *wished* she knew where he was. It did not occur to her son to let her know, nor to her to institute inquiries once she learned he had left Vienna. So while Helver Trebourne, now Duke of Saymore, though he did not know it, frittered away his time chatting to Napoleon and jauntering to this and that foreign city trying out their wine, horses and women, Tisbury and the Duchess shook their heads and declared it was just like him. When he finally strayed back to the Hall nearly eighteen months later, it was to be met with the intelligence that he was now fatherless, a duke, the head of the House of Saymore, lord of three vast estates and their combined incomes, and what was he going to do about the roof, eh?

It was to this last irrelevancy that he asked, with his head reeling, "What?"

"The *roof*, Helver. It has been leaking for months," his mother nagged in an accusing tone. "The upstairs chambers all awash and the maids all sleeping in the good guest rooms. Oh dear!" The chagrined expression that flew to her face was due to this troublesome propinquity of a dozen lively wenches to her lusty son. Not that a flight of stairs would stop him!

"When?" he asked, trying to assimilate the dreadful news.

"Two months ago, at least," she said, frowning with the effort of memory. Helver was only twenty-four, but his mother had been middle-aged when she bore him; and with the burden of such a son, she had become an old woman. Her hair was snow white and a secret source of pride to her. Her eyes were a faded blue, and her face well lined.

"Why are you not in mourning?" he asked, glancing at her grey gown.

"What, for a roof? Don't be foolish. I am just out of mourning for your father."

"You said two months ago," the confused man answered.

"The *roof* took to leaking on us two months ago. Something must be done about it. It has seeped through the ceiling of the green suite, and your Aunt Sara has had to be moved into the blue suite. She hates blue. It makes her bilious."

The heartless youth paid no heed to this calamity but persisted instead to ask his mama about his father's passing. She could hardly recall the details, except that he had a very nice funeral, with two cabinet ministers down from London for the occasion. Time was nothing to her, and it seemed eons since she had had her husband nagging at her across the breakfast table. It was his unpleasant custom to chew out his wife and son at every meal. He had been a hard man to live with, but like most husbands, he had improved considerably with death. It was her custom to speak of him in hushed tones in the village and to remember only his two good points: he had taken marvelous care of his properties, and he had not been a tight-fisted man. But to her son no such feigned reverence was necessary and she spoke quite brusquely.

"Nothing can be done about that. He is dead and buried these eighteen months. What you must do is speak to your man of business about getting some money. He will give me nothing but a pittance, and roofers must be paid. You really must get some money from Buskin and fix the roof, Helver. Well, I daresay you would like a glass of nègus," she said, to make him welcome home from his travels.

Helver went in a trance to her private parlour and sat benumbed at the news of his father's death. A deep frown settled on his handsome brow and his hands dangled between his knees.

"A year and a half — a whole eighteen months! Mama, why didn't you let me know?" he asked.

"Why didn't you come home and you *would* have known," was her unanswerable reply. "Where were you anyway? Here, try the negus," she said, to let him know she cared for him still, even if he was a reprobate and hadn't bothered to come sooner.

He pushed the glass aside, and his mama rather thought she remembered then that Helver didn't care for negus. "It's very good. Cook put nutmeg in it," she told him.

"Thank you, Mama, but I have never cared for lemon juice in my wine, nor nutmeg either. What caused his death?"

"God caused it, of course! The Lord giveth and the Lord taketh away."

After a good deal of discussion, Helver discovered that the Lord had given an ague and taken away his father; and he discovered very little else, except that the roof leaked.

Fatigued from his trip and saddened at the news of his father's death, Helver went to his room to think. So far as he could see, it had not been touched since his leaving, except for a casual dusting. His riding crop still lay on the edge of his dresser, a handful of coins at its side, a pair of topboots kicked under a chair. On his bedside table there was a little note from his neighbour, Edith Durden, wishing him a bon voyage. "I hope you have a wonderful trip, Helver, and don't get in too many scrapes. I will miss you." If she had missed him, she was one of very few who had. He lay down on the bed and crossed his arms over his eyes.

He remembered the scores of times he had caused his father pain, and the equal number of times he had been forgiven with hardly a cross word spoken. His father chewed and jawed about little nothings — a new jacket or waistcoat — but never lit into him over his real transgressions. Yet despite that unending kindness he had never felt close to his father nor, truth to tell, liked him very much. He was the last person applied to in difficulty, and never for advice before committing an indiscretion. He liked his mother better for all her silliness and preoccupation with religion. They had neither of them seemed much like parents. He had really been raised by Travers, his mama's companion who was turned into a nursemaid and then a nanny for those few years when one was required, and a friend for the rest of his life. It was Travers who bound his wounds, who sat with him after having a bone set or during the heat of a fever, who mended his clothes before Mama discovered they were rent and pretended she forgot to tell him to take the pears to the Vicar to save him a scolding. She had written to him at Oxford warning him his father was planning to shoot his favourite mount, only because it had nipped a groom. Poor old Travers, he must go and see her before he went to bed.

A wave of pity for himself, his father, his mother — he hardly knew who — washed over him, and he crawled off the bed to go to Travers to be comforted. He was considered a man's man, but he always felt better, more civilized, when there was a woman around and especially when he was blue. Her room was next to his mother's and he found her there, as he always had, mending, as she always was.

"Still at it, Travers," he said, smiling. "The whole world would fall apart at the seams if you ever stopped mending."

"Helver! Helver, you've come home at last!" she ran to him with tears of gladness in her eyes and threw her arms around him.

He lifted her off her feet and swung her around, as she used to do to him twenty years ago. "The prodigal returns," he said, touched at her joyful reception. Here in Travers's little room was home. Here with this lace-capped lady of the bluebell eyes and hawk nose he was himself — Helver Trebourne and not "that Helver" as he was to the rest of the family.

"Have you missed me, Travers?" he asked, setting her on her feet.

"Does the sky miss the sun?" she asked, urged to an unusual fit of poetry at seeing his dear face.

"The sky might, but I don't think the mother did," he answered.

"Ah, she did, Helver. We all did." She pulled him in, gave him the best chair by the window, petted and cossetted him and told him all the things he couldn't find out from his mother. All the sad details of his father's passing and the duties awaiting him.

"I've been such a disappointment to them," he said. "Such an *awful* son. What's the matter with me? I mean to do better, Travers, truly I do."

"Of course you will," she answered confidently. Looking at his guilt-ridden face, she believed it. But then she had always believed there was good stuff in Helver, if only he hadn't been born to two fools old enough to be his grandparents. A mother who preached religion and worshipped comfort, and a father who despised his son for being the devil-may-care rascal he had made him. Why must they keep the boy home instead of sending him to school like a normal person? No one to chum around with, and when he got older,

11

nothing to do. Not trustworthy enough to handle any of the estates — oh, no. Not an iota of responsibility must be given to him, in case he wouldn't have time to run himself into one scrape after another. Be sure to let him know, after he fooled them and was accepted into Oxford in spite of their efforts to keep him ignorant, that he was expected to fail, or worse. Never give the boy a word of encouragement, but only shake their heads and say by their looks, what next? How will you top this scandal? Oh, no, he hadn't *failed* them; he had done exactly as they expected, and turned out a ne'er-do-well.

But there was time yet to reclaim him. Only twenty-four. The old Duke hadn't expected to go for another ten years, when the boy would be well and truly ruined. She supposed she was being too hard on them. Hel (so well named) had been a rowdy little boy, and they too old to know what to do with him. They mistook every childish prank, shooting a pigeon or chasing a pig, as signs of criminality and gave him the notion he was a scoundrel. And when he started to grow into a young man, what must they do but fill his pockets with gold, saying wisely between themselves that if they didn't keep his purse well filled, he'd take to robbery! Helver, who rode all the way back to the village when the woman at the sweet shop had given him a shilling too much change!

They chatted for a long time, and when finally he arose to go, she said, "You'll do just fine as the Duke, Helver. I'm always here if you need me."

"Why couldn't you be forty years younger, Travers, so I could marry you? I don't want ever to lose you."

"Oh, you can do better than an old lady like me. What we must do now is find you a nice wife. Your flirts won't like it, but they can't be depended on. They've all been getting married off while you were away, you know."

"*All?*" he asked with a teasing smile. "I'll have to turn off half my tenant farmers and bring in some new blood if that's the way they've been cutting up behind my back."

A pretty little maid hustled past, casting a welcoming smile on the new master, and the look was returned with interest. Travers drew in a breath and surmised that Helver's resolutions to do better had not quite firmed up yet. "She's engaged to one of the grooms," she mentioned casually.

"I'm just looking, Travers. Jealous?" he asked, and strolled back to his room.

CHAPTER
TWO

Some three miles west of the Duke of Saymore's sprawling palace there nestled a homey Tudor mansion whose owner would not have exchanged it for the grandest palace in the land. It dated from the late fourteen hundreds and was of that beautiful stone yellowed with the minutest of vegetable matter accumulated over the centuries to turn the stone tawny. The windows were mullioned and leaded, the door a slab of oak five inches thick embedded with metal studs to reinforce it. It was ornamented by no gables, columns or pediments but stood in its original splendour, soaking up sun, rain and history and reflecting somehow both the elements and the past in its pure lines. The Tudor atmosphere prevailed inside as well as out. No modern furniture or pictures were allowed to intrude in this den of antiquity. There was a Gothic spirit prevailing in the main hall, not Gothic run mad with finials and gargoyles, but the woodwork was panels in frames with some modest carving decorating the arches. The furnishings were heavy and not of a sort to encourage their being moved about. Cook had to fight to boil her water in a closed pan, and the joints were still roasted over an open fire in the middle of the kitchen. It was not unknown for the owner, Mrs Durden, who termed herself Dame Durden after the Tudor fashion, to have a pig or calf roasted in her main room in the massive fireplace that could have roasted a horse without crowding.

Dame Durden's chief delight was to live in the past. She outfitted herself in heavily embroidered, wide-sleeved gowns and possessed, though she only wore them in her boudoir, a pair of yellow silk bags with puffed toes that were the footgear of a lady from her favourite period. One of her few compromises with the century in which she lived was to use a fork at the table, but her knife at least she wore on her, like a good Tudor. She winced every time she saw a man use a handkerchief — newfangled contraption — and denigrated any male who wore a beard unless he had earned it by right of soldiering or advanced years. Her servants accepted her strange ways for, other than Cook, they were not much discommoded by them.

She was considered a little strange in the village, but she drove a two-horse carriage, she had a coat of arms, she was an educated lady active in the church and the Historical Society, she shopped locally and paid cash, and so she was accepted. They took her in much the same spirit as Farmer Stokes's three-legged hen, which was also a good layer — with a little suspicion, a little laugh at her eccentricity and a grudging recognition of her worth. She was mentioned with a kind of shameful pride to visitors as Dame Durden of Durden Court, a Tudor home mentioned in all the guide books of Wiltshire.

Dame Durden was a widow and she lived with her one child, a daughter named Edgitha. Dissatisfied with the plain Marys and Elizabeths of Tudor days, the Dame had reached further into the past for a name for her child. Reverting deeper into the past was not despised in intangible matters such as a name. The queen of Edward the Confessor was good enough for the Dame, and she borrowed her name for the child. The modern Georgianas and Arabellas were anathema to her; and, in fact, she made it a point to call Georgiana Hartford Miss George, to show the family her opinion of such made-up names. The name Edgitha, being so odd and difficult of pronunciation, had dwindled to Edith on all occasions except those that required a signature.

Edith had more trials to bear than her name. Unlike her mama, she did not enjoy being pointed out as a quiz when she went to the village. Also, she would have liked to go more often to Tisbury, for she and her mother were fairly isolated at the Court. But running into the village was not encouraged by the Dame. Edith had been educated at home by her mother, had never gone away to even the village school. She hadn't a single friend but her mama and the servants. Her mother fared a little better, but she sheltered Edith from too close a connection with common people, lest the mothers' sons get ideas about marrying her. In short, Edith was lonely, with that gnawing loneliness of the young, waiting for their lives to begin.

In the main drawing room at Durden Court, Edith sat mending a tapestry with her mother. There was a deal of mending and patching done at the Court, to hang on to the dear relics of the past. Edith's curls were not done up in a metal woven caul like her Tudor mother's, but dressed neatly in a bun that had a Tudorish look to it all the same. Her face, too, might have come from a painting of the period. It was a little ivory oval of a face, with dark, serious eyes and a mouth that looked sad in repose but could tilt up mischievously when she was amused. She was not amused now.

"April fifteenth," Dame Durden said. "It will seem odd not to be holding our May Day celebration." An accusing brow was lowered at her daughter at this sad sentence. The reason it was not to be held was that Edith, though usually a compliant enough daughter, had dug in her heels and refused to be made a laughingstock by perching on a hay wagon to ride through the roads. At eighteen last year, she had become quite adamant in the matter. It was her first attempt at setting up her back against any of her mother's schemes, and since that time she had begun to develop a streak of self-determination that was extremely unattractive in the Dame's view. The present bone of contention between them was in the matter of a husband for Edith. What they considered eligible varied widely. For the Dame, the blood in the veins was of paramount importance; but, for the daughter, it was the flesh outside the veins that mattered more, and, of course, a pleasant disposition. They neither of them gave more than the necessary passing thought to material considerations. The Durdens were not fabulously wealthy, but they had more than a competence.

"This will be the second year we have not held it. You must be getting used to the idea, Mama."

"It is a shame to let the good old customs die out. No more cock-fights on Shrove Tuesday, no bonfires on Midsummer-eve, no white garlands hung over the lintels, no handball played for tansy cakes on Easter. Young ladies will next be taking into their heads not to get married." These former gay revels were known to the Dame only through books, and it was really the last-named tradition that she wished to introduce for discussion.

"I don't see any sign of that custom dying out, at least," her daughter answered, choosing to make it a matter of general mores.

"It seems to be dying out in this house," her mother said, getting to the point. "There is Doctor Thorne dangling after you any time this twelve-month with never a word of encouragement for his pains."

"I cannot like him, Mama."

"Not like him? My dear, your wits are gone begging. He traces his ancestors back to Earl Alfgar in the Saxon period, with never a drop of Norman blood in the entire family."

"I wish he had a little Norman blood to warm him up," Edith replied and refused to glance up to receive the withering eye she knew to be turned on her at this heresy.

"A minister of the Church of England doesn't want warm blood," she was told. "You forget Dorion Thorne received his doctorate degree at Oxford last year with a double first. A highly educated and eligible gentleman."

"And you forget, Mama, he has not yet found a living."

"He won't be long being offered a post. Why, the Tisbury living is vacant these six months. I shouldn't doubt he'll be offered that."

"He won't be offered it till Helver gets home," Edith replied, for the living was one belonging to the Duke of Saymore.

"Why, he is home! Did I not tell you?"

The Dame knew perfectly well she had not told Edith this startling piece of news. In their dull lives the weekly visit of the higgler with his game and produce was talked about for hours, and the arrival back at the Hall of Helver would be discussed for weeks. Edith had not been told because her mother strongly desired to see her engaged before any visits with Helver took place. Like every mother with a nubile daughter, she was frightened witless of Helver Trebourne; yet his return could not be kept a secret, so she mentioned it in this seemingly casual fashion. Edith's face lit up like the sun.

"Home? When?" she shouted and leapt from her chair, her end of the tapestry going to the floor.

"Sally told me this morning. She's seeing one of the grooms from the Hall. He got back yesterday. He's been to Elba to see Napoleon, the bounder. Can you beat that? He'll be dashing off to Saint Helena next, no doubt, to resume the friendship."

"I wager he will! It sounds just like him."

"Indeed it does," the Dame said sharply, and wondered that it should throw her daughter into such a paroxysm of joy. She foresaw a very bad spring developing. "He was always partial to Napoleon, and he calls himself an Englishman. Well, he's part French himself, if it comes to that. The second Duchess was a Norman, and blood will tell in the end. What a trial that boy has been to his poor parents. Still, as he is back, he will be appointing a Vicar, and I shouldn't be surprised to see Doctor Thorne chosen."

It was the Dame's firm resolve that as soon as Dorion Thorne got a post, he would marry Edith. She was nineteen years old and in need of a husband to settle her down. She was becoming very restless of late. Only natural that at her age she would be wanting to have a home of her own, a husband and a family. The Dame herself had been married at seventeen, and a mother at Edith's age.

Edith frowned at her mother's statement, for the views held by her parent were no secret from her. She, too, wanted to marry and leave Durden Court; but any gentleman she could care for at all was instantly castigated as a mongrel by her mother. Whatever the actual pedigree, the blood was not considered blood in any genealogical sense by Dame Durden if the true Saxon ichor was polluted by a Norman strain. And if the family could not be traced without a break to the tenth century, it was automatically assumed the records had been destroyed to conceal the taint of the Normans. She did at least give people credit for wanting to *appear* to have blood. But the matter of breeding aside, Edith found that when a gentleman was full of admirable qualities such as brains, manners and propriety, she could admire him, but she could not love him. She suspected, too, that the reason for this oddity on her part was that she loved Helver Trebourne, whom she did not admire in the least for any worthy qualities. Indeed, she knew only too well he hadn't a worthy quality to his name.

Despite the five years age difference, the chasm of their social positions and their sexes, they had been much together in their youth. Both educated at home and no other youngsters living nearby, they had met in the fields that separated the two estates and become friends. All summer long they would ride together over the fields chasing rabbits and picking flowers, building a tree house and wading in the creek, spearing loaches. They discovered a marvelous cave and imagined themselves primitive creatures who had to store up every rock in the fields for their protection. Helver taught a young Edith how to make a fire from stones and straw, only it never lit for either of them. They once planned to run away together to join a monastery in France, for in this halcyon past it had not occurred to either of them that Edith was a female. In fact, she was called Eddie by Helver. When the fact that she wore skirts, and occasionally had to be pulled across a stream or up a rock *did* occur to him, their easy meetings were about over. A young girl on the verge of womanhood was not allowed to roam the countryside with a buck whose reputation as a rakeshame was beginning to flourish. They were then together only infrequently, and usually under the eyes of some chaperone. But the friendship of their youth was a strong bond and there was no feeling of strangeness between them when Helver left. They still occasionally met by chance in the three miles of land between their homes, three-quarters of which belonged to the Saymores though it was used for riding by Edith, and there in that neutral territory they could resume their interrupted friendship.

"Did you *really* kidnap Peg Watkins?" a saucer-eyed Edith, now twelve, would ask, vastly impressed.

"Not kidnapped exactly. I was rescuing her," the worldly seventeen-year-old explained condescendingly. "They're going to send her to Buxtons to be a dairymaid, and Peg's put in a panic by cows. Only that mugger of a tutor of mine got bitten by his horse and let out such a bellow he woke the whole town and landed in the roundhouse."

"What were you going to do with her?"

"I thought your mama might like her to tend the chickens, Eddie. She's awfully pretty. Or I would have looked after her myself."

"How?"

"I had lots of ideas, only they've sent her off to Buxtons. She doesn't have a pair of shoes, Eddie. Imagine that! I bought her a pair, and she was afraid to take them home. She used to put them on and dance — out behind the church, you know. At least she has a pair of shoes to take to Buxtons."

Later the question was, "Did you *really* beat up your tutor at Oxford, Helver?" A "really" was necessary, for one could not quite credit that a sane man or boy had performed such acts.

"Oh, *beat him up*! Is that what they're saying? It was only a tap on the cheek to make him accept my challenge. Called me a bloody pedant because I corrected him on a few points. He was only angry I knew more Greek than he did. Mind you, if I'd known what he meant I might not have done it, but I thought he was insulting me. Anyway, I'd have liked to have a duel. I wouldn't have *killed* him."

"Did they expel you just for that?"

"I'm not expelled, just sent down for the rest of the term. But I don't intend to go back. The Bagwig took to raking me down for being impertinent to that dashed tutor, and, once you're in *his* bad books, you're for it. So I left before they kicked me out. Well, Papa never thought I'd get in at all, so I guess he ain't much surprised. I'm not the first of my clan not to graduate. At least I got in, that's something."

How was it possible for a young girl *not* to fall in love with such a rapscallion as this, especially when he was so exquisitely handsome? He was Eddie's hero, and he looked exactly as a hero should look. Eyes so dark brown they were nearly black, and a tanned complexion that gave him the air of a Corsair. He had an interesting series of mishaps that decorated his body with an assortment of black eyes, bruises, limps and other irresistible allurements. And then, in their last meetings, he had become very thoughtful, bringing her a little book of French poetry that she couldn't half understand, but she could see it related to "amour." He had helped her scamper up a tree so the bailiff wouldn't see her and tell her mama, and warned her against the day when she should find herself in love. At the time he was in love himself with the Widow Malone. He informed Eddie she would know when she was in love by being so miserable she couldn't eat or sleep or do a thing but think of the face of the loved one. Taking his word for gospel, she had realized that night she was in love with Helver, for she was sick with jealousy and lay awake for hours thinking of him and the Widow. He protected her from imaginary lechers who would try to make her drunk by smuggling a bottle of claret to the meadow, without drinking glasses, for her to become accustomed to its vile effects. He later brought a medicine bottle of brandy, but she was only allowed to smell this so she'd recognize the smell when it was offered to her.

She knew he was not quite a proper person, and, of course, she never heard a good word spoken of him either at home or abroad. He was "that Helver Trebourne," who was killing his parents with his carryings-on, and one could not admire him; yet it was he and no other that she loved. If it was inevitable that she should love him, it was similarly inevitable that one of his bent for the dramatic should not find anything in her to cherish. There was no romance in a little girl you had grown up with. She required no rescuing from a wicked step-mother or guardian. She had no secret past to excite the curiosity, no foreign accent or graces to please the senses, no heroine's face or form to inflame the libido. She was just Eddie Durden, whose only charm was in her familiarity and lack of criticism.

Like the sensible girl she was and knowing her feelings to be hopeless, Edith came to realize as she matured that her best course was to marry. When Doctor Thorne had singled her out for attentions, she had been flattered. He was well thought of, a very learned man, and would make an unexceptionable husband once he got a position. It was said by everyone that he was going places. He made himself agreeable to all persons in a position to do him a favour, and his easy manners, combined with his intelligence and education, made even a bishopric before he was fifty something not beyond him. His opinion of himself outdid that held by the world. He intended to be a bishop before he was forty. A rising churchman needed a wife of impeccable background and adequate fortune; and a young gentleman of some human proclivities preferred also that she be neither old nor ugly, nor totally devoid of sense and humour. After carefully writing down a balance sheet of all the local ladies with their credits and debits, Doctor Thorne found Miss Durden to have more to offer than any other and decided to marry her. He was not unaware that she showed no great partiality for him; but an assiduous courting of the Dame and long discussions of their genealogical charts had assured him of the mother's wholehearted support in his quest. He was not despairing of marrying Edith as soon as he got a post.

Edith knew well he was looking in her direction, but, even while she was flattered, she was afraid. Afraid she would have to take him, whether she wanted to or no. He looked very noble in the pulpit, where he occasionally made a guest appearance in Tisbury. He had a thin face, burning eyes and a well-shaped nose. He was strict and forceful with the parishioners, and a good speaker. Out of the pulpit, she liked him less. Least of all did she admire him in motion. He did not walk like a man should. He had a creeping, flat-footed, shuffling sort of a walk. His heels did not strike the ground first as a man's should, as did Helver Trebourne's, for example. He made no sound when he moved. He could slip up behind you in church or in a shop and lay a hand on your arm before you realized he was there. She thought of it as a dishonest, sneaking kind of a walk. It was the least appealing thing about him, yet it was foolish not to like a good man because of the way he walked. There was much to admire in Doctor Thorne.

CHAPTER
THREE

Helver had been home for three days, and twice a day he thought of Eddie Durden — when he went to bed at night and saw her little note on his bedside table, and when he arose in the morning and saw it again. He rather wanted to go and see her for, with Travers, she formed what he considered his real family, and he was eager to tell her about his trip. But he had not been made welcome at Durden Court since he had become a man. In his youth he had been there on many a cold day, sliding down bannisters, eating Tudor treats, reading the Dame's books and drawing pictures. It was around the time of his involvement with the Widow Malone, his first public love affair, that he had been hinted away. He supposed the foolish old Dame thought he had designs on Eddie.

It was Travers who urged him to go and see her. She was the only soul besides Edith herself who hoped to promote a marriage in that quarter. She was leery to see how that sassy chit of a Mary Gordon, the upstairs maid engaged to the groom, was rolling her eyes at him. But that would be only a vexation if he should start carrying on with her. Worse trouble loomed in the village in the form of a new widow that Helver did not appear to have yet run into. Fortunately, he was so busy about the estate he had not spent much time in Tisbury. A marriage would be the making of him, and a careful consideration of all the ladies in the neighbourhood had thrown up Edith Durden as the best match, so Travers asked him one day if he had seen Eddie yet.

"No, I suppose she's still at the Court?"

"Indeed she is, and she must be dying of curiosity to hear all about your trip. Why don't you drop over and pay her a call? The Dame doesn't come here, you know."

"I know it well, and she don't much care for me to go there, either."

"She'll let you call, now that you're a duke. She isn't that big a gudgeon."

"I'm surprised the people who are smiling at me these days. Bathurst came posting all the way down from London to see me. He wants to make sure I'm in the Tory camp, of course."

"I suppose you sent him off with a flea in his ear?"

"No, I was very civil to him, and didn't wear my white hat, either. I expect I'll become a Tory one of these days, like Papa. And the Dean of Salisbury came, too. Imagine, *me* receiving cabinet ministers and divines! What is the world coming to, Travers?" He looked as pleased as punch at these routine calls.

With a gentle insistence, Travers pointed out that there were three hours to dinner, and, if he hustled off before anyone else came to see him, he would have time for a cose with Edith.

The Dame was at a meeting of the Historical Society in Tisbury, and so Helver was not only admitted to the Court but allowed to stay an hour with Edith without so much as a chaperone. He found her staring into the grate, in which three quarters of an elm tree roared its flames up the flue, and it wasn't even cold out. There was a book beside her, but her hands were empty and her mouth down-turned.

He walked in unannounced and stopped at the door to look at her. What a quaint little creature she was — hadn't changed a bit.

"I'm home from the wars once again!" he declared, smiling.

Her eyes widened and lit up. She jumped up, sending the book flying, and ran to him. "Oh, Helver, did you *really* go to Elba and see Napoleon?" she asked, before even making him welcome.

"Certainly I did."

"I wager you helped him escape," she said, and meant it.

"Indeed I did not! You can admire an individual without sympathizing with his principles."

"I know," she said, a quick picture of Doctor Thorne flashing into her head.

"I still think him the greatest general of our time."

"Well, Wellington beat him at Waterloo."

"Wellington and Blucher and the rest of Europe put together. It took their combined forces and a good deal of bungling on the part of his own generals . . . But that is nothing to the point. I am happy he is beaten, once for all."

He settled himself on an unpadded Tudor saddle seat before the fire and glanced to his companion.

"What were you doing the rest of the time?" Edith asked eagerly.

"Booting around here and there."

"Have you any new scars to show me?" A regular part of their clandestine meetings in the fields was for Helver to show off the various damages he had suffered in his exploits.

"No, but I fell into the Mediterranean. I was standing talking with Napoleon and a bunch of fellows, on a high cliff, too, and my foot slipped and I went tumbling right into the sea. Boney laughed as if he'd split his sides, but I wasn't hurt. The Mediterranean is dandy to swim in, nice and warm. Talking about warm," he said, moving back his saddle seat and running a finger around his collar, "the Dame would love it in Spain. As hot as an oven."

"Did you go to Spain?"

"I spent three months there, becoming familiar with the flora and fauna. Especially the fauna."

"I thought it was the Floras you'd be becoming familiar with."

"Ignoramus! Hasn't the Dame taught you anything? The flora are the flowers, and the fauna are the animals."

"What animals do they have in Spain?"

"Not a decent horse in the whole country as far as I can see, and Italy was worse. They have the devil of a lot of oxen and swine. They cook the pork up very tender, too. In one place the waiter sliced up a suckling pig with a plate, just for show, you know. But their most outstanding fauna are their women. Dark eyes and lovely complexions." His eyes took on a dreamy, reminiscent look.

"You look Spanish yourself, or Italian maybe. Latin, I mean."

"I'm devilish glad I ain't. You'll never guess how they run things in Italy, Eddie. You can't get next or nigh single girls."

"You'd never minded groups before, Helver."

He looked to see if she was roasting him and saw it to be the case. He reached out and chucked her chin. "Brass box. The Dame hasn't succeeded in teaching you any manners, either. I thought you'd grow up into a nice little prude. How did you get so saucy? You should show a little respect to your elders. I'm a duke now, you know."

"I know. You don't seem like one. Should I be calling you 'Your Grace,' or genuflecting, or kissing your hand or something to show my respect?"

"Oh, if you want to be kissing me, never mind the hands. That's for cardinals, or Popes. But you could quit joshing me, you hussy. I had Bathurst and a Dean from Salisbury to call, and they both treated me with more respect than you are. It'll take me a few years to grow my hair grey and my spine stiff. I daresay it will come in time. But I was going to tell you how they manage their women. If you ask one to meet you somewhere, alone, I mean, for — well, you know . . ."

"For *amor* — isn't that what they call it in Italian?"

"You've learned that much anyway, I see!" he said, laughing his old, easy laugh. "It's hard to get one of them to slip away from her chaperone — they're guarded something terrible. You have to slip them a note by their maids, and in Italian, too. The best place to spot them is the churches. I saw a lot of nice churches. What they'll do is tell you that *after they're married* they'll be very happy to have you for a lover! Can you beat that? *After* they're married. I wouldn't be an Italian husband for anything. There isn't a one among them has a faithful wife. It's a form of disgrace if a wife don't have a lover on the side. I was never so shocked. They don't mean widowed, either. I wasted weeks trailing after a doe-eyed widow in Florence. They mean that when they have a husband living, they'll take a lover. A widow is no more free than a single girl. The only girls worth making up to in Italy are married. Really, I don't think it's worth the price. You're a *cavaliere servente*, as they call it, but more *servente* than *cavaliere*. You're expected to have only one *amarosa* at a time, and wait on her hand and foot. Running errands for her, and wasting time at operas and concerts and *conversazione* where the women all huddle at one end of the room and you're stuck to stand around drinking rotten wine with men at the other. And for all you hear so much about their opera, they none of them listen to a note. They take their playing cards to their boxes and play cards and talk and flirt and don't pay the least notice to the singers. I thought it was awfully rude of them, but the singers don't seem to mind."

"Was the trip a complete waste of time, then, as far as the fauna went?"

"Oh, I wouldn't say that!" he answered with a smile. "The *cavaliere servente* is pretty well paid for his work. But for my money you can keep their fine ladies. The middle-class girls have it all over them for looks, and availability, too. And the husbands don't seem at all jealous. You never hear of a duel. Though quite a bit of beating up goes on in dark alleys," he said, rubbing a shoulder that seemed still to bother him after all these months. Eddie assumed it had received a good clubbing in some dark alley and smiled at him.

"Lucky they're not jealous," she said.

"Well, I would sure be jealous if I was married to one of them. They are smashing-looking women. But no prettier than Dame Durden's daughter," he finished up with a bow.

"I see you've learned some fine Italian manners. You didn't used to bother letting on you thought I was pretty."

He subjected her to a close scrutiny. "You're coming along, now I take a good look at you," he said mildly. "What have you been doing with yourself now I'm not here to keep an eye on you?"

"Oh, falling in love and breaking hearts and becoming bitter and disillusioned and things," she answered airily, to repay him for being a *cavaliere servente*.

"How interesting! A new idea for you, Eddie, to be setting up as a *femme fatale*. I'll be falling in love with you myself if you keep this up. Tell me all about it."

"I must have my little secrets. An air of mystery is part of the bag of tricks of a *femme fatale*, is it not?"

"Yes, but a brown bombazine gown ain't. Don't try to gull *me* you've been breaking any hearts in that granny gown, with your hair all screwed to your head in a ball like your mother. The girls in Italy wear it out loose. It looks lovely. I suppose the truth of the matter is the Dame has chosen a squire for you, has she?"

"No, she's only been trying to, but I'll choose for myself one of these days."

"In other words, you're growing up on me. I don't think I like that." He looked hard at her, but she didn't seem much different than she had when he left, only a little prettier maybe. Something about the eyes.

"A young lady either grows up or dies, and I don't care much for the latter alternative."

"You could stay the same. I should have put a rock on your head before I left to stop you from growing. Now I suppose if I call on you or take you out for a drive, people will say I'm courting you."

"How horrid for you! You'll have to bring along Aunt Sara for a chaperone to protect your reputation till I'm married. Then you can be my *cavaliere servente*."

"It was *your* reputation I was thinking of. And the Dame would be the worst of the lot. All the old biddies whisper behind their fans every time I wink at a girl or offer to carry her parcels."

"Or slip her behind a door for a kiss. The old biddies do carry on so about nothing. It's quite shocking!" she roasted him.

"Yes, and they'll be worse than ever now I'm a duke. Uncle Egbert is already at me to get buckled, and Travers, too. Can you imagine *me married?*"

"No, I can't imagine it at all," she said truthfully.

"It's the worst fate in the world for a man, to be stuck with one woman forever. I don't know what induces all the fellows to plunge ahead and do it."

"It seems Mama was right in her predictions," Eddie laughed. "Only the other day she was bemoaning the passing of the old ways — the May Day revels and so on. She prophesied marriage would be the next thing to go by the boards."

"Are you not having your May Day celebration this year?"

"No, we didn't have it last year, either. I refused to get myself rigged out in a bunch of flowers and be borne aloft on the haywagon to be pulled through the roads, making a fool of myself. Mama wanted to make Sally do it, but she threatened to quit."

"I always liked the Dame's May Day revels. You looked very nice in that white dress, too, Eddie, with your hair out loose for a change. I was looking forward to it. And if you beat the quintain, you get to kiss the Queen of the May, too. A peck on the cheek, if you can call that a kiss."

"You never beat the quintain yet but got hit on the back with the sack of flour every time you tried it, so I don't suppose you would have beat it this year, either."

"Still, there are lots of other opportunities at your May Day celebrations. The Tudor gentlemen knew what they were about. I think I might have worked one kiss in."

"You used to work in quite a few of them. There was Hettie, that you took into the barn to show the five-legged calf that you'd pinned a stuffed white stocking on to make up the fifth leg. And there was Dorrit . . ."

"Lord, how do you remember all my past sins? That was years ago. But it wasn't a Hettie or a Dorrit I was talking about this year. It was an Eddie," he said with a smile. Helver didn't even consider such a polite conversation as this a flirtation, but he began to realize from her blushes that Eddie had changed. Instead of telling him she'd empty the quintain bag of flour over his head if he tried it, as he expected she would, she was blushing.

"Lord, Eddie, I hope you're not going to go all missish on me. I was only fooling, you know."

"I know."

"A fellow has to have someone he can talk foolishly to. They've been ragging at me at home about seeing bailiffs and making appointments and fixing the roof and all sorts of things till my head aches. I came here to relax."

"Tell me some more about your trip, Helver," Eddie said, to soothe him into a good humour and relax him. He entertained her for an hour with stories better kept to himself, then left, as he was not anxious to run into the Dame.

He didn't escape her by much. The Dame had a view of his back riding home to the Hall as she came in her

36

carriage up the lane. When she got into the living room, she asked Edith about the visit at once.

"He came over to tell us about his trip," Edith explained, knowing she had done wrong in her mama's eyes to let him stay so long. As he was now Duke of Saymore, no stern lecture was read.

"It was civil of him to call. I'm sorry I missed his visit," her mother surprised her by saying. "But I trust he won't make a practice of it. What had he to say?"

That he had been to the Congress of Vienna and to Elba to see Napoleon was brushed aside as no news, and that he had been busy chasing girls in four countries was, of course, not mentioned. "Did he mention the living at Tisbury?" the Dame enquired.

"No, he didn't mention that," Edith replied. Talking to Helver was never so down-to-earth as that.

"And *you* didn't mention it to him! What were you thinking of? He will be giving it to Hanley Barton or one of his loose friends if we don't put the notion in his head. If he comes again, be sure to mention Doctor Thorne is looking for a post."

"He didn't mention coming again," Edith said. This, at least, was welcome news and received no rancourous return.

CHAPTER
FOUR

A few days passed without Helver returning to the Court, and the Dame's suspicions were somewhat abated. It had long been Edith's custom to ride in the track of land between her home and Helver's, and she saw no reason to discontinue doing so. In fact, she was there rather more often than she used to be; but, with the fine spring weather to lure a girl outdoors, her mama did not tumble to it that her daughter's rides had any other end than air and exercise. On her next outing Edith achieved her real goal and ran into Saymore. It was mid-afternoon and he was returning from some rounds with his bailiff, mounted on a fine bay stallion. He saw her from some distance and waved a hand and shouted to her. She reined in to wait for him.

"Hello, Eddie," he said, "what have you been doing with yourself? Playing *femme* fatale to all your suitors?"

"That's right. I just rode out for a bit to get rid of them," she answered smiling. She hadn't seen a soul but her mother, the servants and Mrs Petrie, who came to help do the milking, since her last visit with Helver.

"You must give me a run-down on the pack. Start with the top dog. What's his name?"

No suitor but Doctor Thorne had ever been allowed to do more than stand up once with Eddie at the local assemblies, and this intimation of a whole slew of men would be difficult to keep up. But at least she could name the top dog without shame. "Doctor Thorne is at the head of the pack," she answered.

"A doctor, eh? I suppose he's a church doctor. One of the local Thornes?"

"Yes, you remember Dorion."

"Ah, Dorion — the purebred, like yourself. You sure the Dame isn't choosing your beau for you? I can't believe *you* are much impressed with his sang-froid, and I mean that to be taken quite literally, as you always do interpret the French idiom, my little cabbage."

"Mama favours him, of course, but he is well thought of hereabouts by everyone."

"Let us say *nearly* everyone. *I* consider him in the nature of a Thorne in the side. I never liked him above half, but maybe that's because he was always held up as a model of perfection to me — going to college on scholarship and nabbing every prize going. I can't imagine what you see in that dull fellow. Shall we get down and walk? I see the yellow sally is running in the creek. I'll pick you some if you like." He threw a leg over the mount's back and hopped down, looking expectantly to Eddie to make her own descent, but she sat waiting for his help.

"Learning all the ladies' tricks, I see," he laughed up at her and raised his arms to help her down. She suddenly felt embarrassed and hesitated a moment, so that he stood looking up at her shy smile; and, when she did jump down, he was aware of the soft feminine feel of her waist between his hands. After her feet touched the ground he held her a moment, looking at her. "I think you've grown," he said. "You didn't used to be up to my chin."

"Yes, I'm taller than Mama now," she replied, and stepped back from him.

He kept looking at her. "You've got — bigger," he said, which sounded a little foolish as she was quite slim. "Filled out, I mean," he enlarged.

"Well, I *am* a girl, Helver," she said, laughing lightly.

"No, you're a woman," he answered, and seemed quite displeased to have discovered it. They walked through the fields, leading their mounts; and, with every tree and hillock recalling some childhood exploit to them, Helver soon forgot the nasty trick Eddie had played him by growing up. He also forgot to pick the yellow sally but remembered more tales from abroad. The creek appeared to remind him of Italy.

"What we need for this is a gondola," he told her.

"A raft, do you mean?" she asked.

"No, a boat, you ignoramus. And a gondolier so we can sit down and talk and make love while he rows us."

"Is that what you did in Spain?"

"It's Italy where you use gondolas. In Venice the pavements are all water."

"Does it rain a lot?"

"There wasn't a speck of rain all the time I was there. Actually, I was only in Venice a week."

"Why don't they put cobblestones down?"

40

"In a canal? Use your head, Eddie. Really, you're as ignorant as a hummingbird. I should take you to Italy and Spain. You'd love it. It's time you discovered what's going on in the world."

"I'd better get married first, don't you think? I wouldn't want to scandalize the Venetians."

"Yes, single ladies don't have any fun. Couldn't we rig up a gondola for this creek, I wonder?" he asked, looking around for logs.

"It's only six inches deep," Eddie reminded him.

He stuck in his boot to the ankle to test it; it was a very fine boot, too, of Cordoba leather, purchased in Spain. "At least we wouldn't drown. Did I tell you about the girl in Venice who pushed me into the canal from our gondola?"

"No."

"No, and I guess I'd best not tell you, either, as the details return to me. Let's tether the horses to a tree and leap across to the other side. There are some nice bluebells there. They'll match your eyes. You don't see many blue eyes in Italy."

"My eyes are grey," Eddie mentioned.

"Are they though? I thought they were blue. Travers's eyes are blue. I must have seen your eyes a thousand times. How unobservant of me. It's pebbles or slate I should be giving you to match them," he said, looking to confirm that indeed they were grey. With the longest lashes he had ever seen anywhere.

"Let's go," he said, and with a leap he was across the creek, with just one foot landing in the water on the other side. "That will teach me to jump off my hocks," he laughed, shaking the water. "Come on, I'll catch you."

"I'll never do it," Eddie answered, looking with some uncertainty at the creek, which was at its highest point in the spring.

"Yes you will. You used to jump it ten years ago when your legs were only half the length they are now. Come on."

Helver had always demanded the impossible of her on their excursions in the meadow. She had been forced up trees whose height terrified her, into caves where the shadows scared her half to death and many times she had been commanded across this same creek. She went back a few steps to give herself a start, daintily lifted her skirts and jumped across it. With a longer start than Helver, she got both feet on to dry land. Helver caught her, though it was not strictly necessary for safety purposes.

"Good girl," he said. But with his hands again on her waist, he was reminded that she was no longer a slip of a girl. And, really, he couldn't think how he came never to have noticed her grey eyes before.

"You can let go now," she said, pushing his hands gently away.

"Oh, yes, I must remember you're not a married lady yet. Too bad," he replied lightly.

"You'd best remember you're back in England, too. Married ladies aren't so available here."

"No, you have to wait around till they're widowed. Though I must say in London the married ladies are not at all untouchable."

Eddie sighed wearily at his indefatigable pursuit of women, but he grabbed her hand and ran off to a nearby field to pick three bluebells and hand them to her. She also picked one, and gave it to him.

"In Spain, you know, when a lady gives you a flower, it's an invitation."

"An invitation to what?" she asked.

"To — nothing."

"That's not much of an invitation, is it?"

"No, I guess not." He looked at Eddie closely and couldn't quite decide whether she was grown up or not. She still had a blunt, childish way of speaking.

"Is it an invitation to *amor?*" she asked, quizzing him.

"Something like that." In the old days she would have been treated to an unexpurgated telling of all his knowledge, but now there was some strangeness between them. He was impatient with it.

"You should have warned me. I think I'll take my flower back."

"No, I'll keep it. You're not getting out of your invitation that easily." He put it in his buttonhole, and they walked on in a silence not so comfortable as it used to be between them till Helver spotted their old cave and had to go in and rediscover it. "Look at the pile of stones. Do you remember we were going to kill dinosaurs with them?"

"And rabbits, to skin and eat," she remembered. "I hate rabbit stew, actually. It makes me sick."

"I was sick as a horse in Florence from eating some bad seafood — flat on my back for a week. I saw the house where Dante lived."

"Dante who?"

"Eddie, don't you know who *Dante* is?"

"No, who is he?" She probably knew more about English history than anyone in Wiltshire except her mother, but she realized that in other matters she had something to learn. Her conversations with Doctor Thorne also made her aware of her ignorance, but with him she could not admit so baldly that she didn't know what he was talking about. Yet he would explain more kindly than Helver, and not say a word to make her *feel* ignorant.

"He was Beatrice's lover," he told her.

"Who is Beatrice?" she asked, unabashed to reveal the full depths of her lack of knowledge.

"They were the greatest pair of lovers ever known."

"You couldn't expect Mama to tell me that! Was he her *cavaliere servente?*"

"No, he was engaged to another lady."

"Can't an engaged man be a *cavaliere?*"

"It wasn't that way with them. It was a real love affair. The kind that only happens once in a century or so."

"It shouldn't happen — except between a man and his wife, I mean."

"You can't control a passion like that. It has nothing to do with marriage — with man-made laws and settlements, and legal papers. It's like some great elemental force that you couldn't combat if you wanted to, and who would want to?"

"*I* would if I were engaged to someone else."

"Well, I wouldn't. I'd give anything to have been Dante. It was worth the trip to Hell and Purgatory and all the rest. I'll try to find you a translation of *The Divine Comedy*. Then you'll understand. It's a poem Dante wrote." Helver had been reading *The Divine Comedy* steadily for a year himself and considered it the greatest thing ever written.

"Good, I like comedies."

"It's a *poem*, Eddie."

"Oh, a holy poem, I suppose. I mean, you said 'divine.'"

"A divine poem — holy, if you like, or a story or an allegory or a mystical explanation of life. It's everything."

"I'm reading Walter Scott's Waverley novels," she offered, to show him her mind was occupied, too; and, despite his enthusiasm for Dante, he had also taken considerable enjoyment from the Wizard of the North and was ready to discuss his works.

Helver kicked a few stones from the pile at the cave's mouth and looked at Edith. "I should be getting back to the Hall. There are usually half a dozen people waiting to see me." This was a new formality between them, for excuses to be necessary. In the past he would just have gone, saying goodbye if he thought of it. But Eddie was a lady now, and he felt some sense of decorum must be maintained. "Shall I ride you home?"

"Oh, no. I'll go alone."

"Did the Dame rip up about my calling the other day?"

"No — no, it's not that."

"I see," he said, and here was something else different. Eddie was lying to him, and he was pretending to believe her. They were becoming polite to each other, like adults, or strangers.

They recrossed the stream at a narrower point where no help was required by Edith. He helped her up into the saddle and stood till she rode off, waving a salute. Everything had changed. The meadow had changed, he had changed and Eddie Durden had changed. He wished things were back as they had been. What he really wished was that he was a boy again, with no group of people waiting to be interviewed, and no responsibilities. He was unhappy as he rode home, even angry — with Eddie, and the world.

Edith cantered rather quickly back to the Court. Her mouth was turned down at the corners. He hadn't changed a bit, she thought. He was still wild, woman-crazy, still thinking she was a child. He didn't even know her eyes were grey, and they had been as close as brother and sister. She knew every line of his face, every scar and every contour. She knew him inside-out.

CHAPTER
FIVE

Helver Trebourne, used to a life of idle dissipation, found that as Duke of Saymore a great change was taking place. Instead of awaking mornings with twenty or so hours to kill, for he never slept much, he had a crowded calendar on his hands. When his father was alive he had never been induced to take any interest in the domain that would one day be his, had no clear idea of how many acres or tenants he had, nor even what was his income. Now he spent his mornings seeing a crowded anteroom of people ranging from office-seekers to tenants with problems and his afternoons with Forringer, his bailiff, riding about the estate to decide on projects. Such arcane matters as tilling fields, trying a new strain of sheep and building new fences were brought to his attention for consideration, and he realized his own ignorance. But Forringer did not despair of making him a good landlord. He was quick to learn the rudiments of farming, swift of eye to see a field lying fallow due to an excess of water, good at figures to realize the profit to be made from spending money on improvements. He was also more daring than the old Duke, ready to try anything and to institute improvements on a grand scale. The tenant farms along the Avon that were slowly sinking into the river would not be jacked up and moved back a dozen yards but rebuilt from scratch in brick, not plaster and wood.

"It'll cost you something," Forringer warned.

"Yes, and a good deal more if we move them this year and they take to crumbling on us in another three. As well do the thing right. I'm richer than I knew."

"Aye, well, the late Duke was an accountant, if you'll pardon my saying so, Your Grace. He had an eye to the interest always. If you invested the difference between moving and building into the funds, you'd be making five percent."

"Which would cover about one-quarter the cost of building in three years' time."

"The costs will be up in three years' time, too, but meanwhile you'll be losing the interest."

"And my tenants gaining decent roofs over their heads. There are rats in those thatched roofs, Forringer. I think I must bring a team down here for a rat hunt. It'll be great fun." Fun was never quite abandoned in his pursuit of duty.

"Her Grace likes the thatched roofs. Gives the place a quaint look, you know."

"Her Grace doesn't have to have rats gnawing their way through her larder." She did, however, have still a leaky roof over her own head, as Helver hadn't gotten around to having it mended.

"We'll go ahead with the brick homes, then?" Forringer asked hopefully.

48

"Yes, get in touch with suppliers and builders and send them around to see me. We'll want to give the work to local people as much as possible."

He came home tired after his outings but with a feeling of quiet satisfaction of a day's work done, to be greeted by his mother, Aunt Sara and her husband, Uncle Egbert, to tell him the men hadn't come to start on the roof, and the fires in the succession houses had been allowed to go out, and the cook's helper must be turned off for she was a thief, stealing the eggs. A dozen short today alone.

"Things weren't let run to rack and ruin when your father was alive," Sara told him.

"That's news to me," Helver returned, thinking of the homes along the Avon where you couldn't step out the front door without wetting your feet.

"What you need is a wife to look after the house," Egbert would add.

"I have a mother, an aunt and an uncle," Helver said shortly. "I should think between them they could see to a thieving servant girl and make sure the fires in the conservatories are kept lit. I suppose the pineapples are ruined, are they?"

"They're not frozen, at least, for it's a warm April," Sara allowed.

After an unpleasant, bickering repast, one or the other of the old crones would bring out the cards and remark how handy it was that Helver was there to make a fourth for whist. An appealing eye to Travers usually worked, and he fled the house to escape their harping and to find a couple of hours' amusement in more congenial company before going to bed. Travers had exaggerated to say *all* his flirts were married. There were still a few around, but it was masculine company in which he spent most of his time. It was soon being reported in the neighbourhood that "that Helver Trebourne" hadn't changed a bit. Had kept the fellows up till three o'clock gambling at the Green Man, and had you heard that the young parlour maid at the Hall was already in trouble? That the fault for this was Helver's had to be denied, but it was seen as an omen of the population increase to be expected soon in the environs. Knowing shakes of the head accompanied these words, and the community sat back to see what he would be up to next. He did not disappoint them.

During his absence on the Continent a character nearly as interesting to the locals as himself had moved into Tisbury. She was the Baroness De Courcy, a youngish widow and a decided dasher. Her beautiful red tresses were brushed back from an alabaster brow; her eyes were large, dark and amorous, and her pouting lips a feature considered obscene by the females but divine by the men. It was as good as a play to see her saunter down the narrow streets of the village, a different parasol every day shielding her face from the sun, and, unfortunately, from half her audience, as well. But she had a cunning way of tilting it to give a view if the approaching feet wore a well-cut pair of topboots or Hessians. Her gowns turned every woman's eye green with envy and every tongue loose with chastisement. Why she had come to a backwater like Tisbury was a subject of infinite conjecture, but, whatever the reason, the result was perfectly obvious. There wasn't a man in the village or for five miles around who didn't spend half his waking hours gawking in front of the apothecary shop across the road from her residence, waiting for her to come or go, and the women weren't much better occupied. They contented themselves to await her presence from behind their lace curtains, for they wouldn't give the bold hussy the satisfaction of letting her know of their interest.

It was the collective wish of the women of the village to have the pleasure of snubbing her, but the wish was not fulfilled. She ignored them. She smiled and spoke to every man or boy with whom she had the slimmest acquaintance, and they had most of them scraped an acquaintance by holding open a door for her or retrieving her pug, who had the habit of slipping his leash when she walked him. It was no secret to the women that she did it on purpose, of course, buckled the pug's collar up loosely so he'd bolt on her. The Baroness was very much aware of the title she bore, and the only females with whom she was on terms were the Duchess of Saymore and her sister, Lady Sara. There was another woman, Jessie Hartman, who was honoured with a nod. Her brother was a successful merchant, reputedly a millionaire, which might have accounted for her recognizing a commoner.

It was as clear as day and as certain as Fate that some major drama would be enacted when "Milady," as the villagers mockingly called Lady De Courcy to cast aspersions on her title, met Helver Trebourne. The curtains were well occupied hiding the women when it was learned that Helver was back at the Hall, for no one wanted to miss the first meeting. It was not quite the passionate affair the onlookers could have wished, but it promised interesting events to follow for it came to light that Milady already knew Helver. It was even conceded by a few of the more charitable that she might *really* be a lady when the acquaintance was discovered.

Helver had ridden into Tisbury to pick up a pair of boots he had ordered before leaving nearly eighteen months ago. He somewhat shared his mother's uninterest in the passing of time. As he walked along the street with the boots under his arm, unwrapped, he spotted Lady De Courcy make her daily exit from her abode and entrance on to the main street. His eyes fastened on her as a hawk's upon first spotting a rabbit, and his feet automatically took him across the road, though he had meant to pick up some peppermint drops for his mama at the apothecary. Peppermint drops, new boots and all other extraneous matters fell from his mind as his eyes travelled along the lines of the modish gown that clung to her equally modish body. The parasol was never opened that day, the first time Milady ever went on the street without its protection. But her eyes were as sharp as Helver's, and she recognized a Weston coat as quickly as he picked out a Parisian gown. No slower was she to notice a broad shoulder and trim waist than he to pinpoint a high bosom and flowing thigh. They advanced towards each other and not a sound was to be heard in any living room but the very slight rustle of the curtains as they were pushed aside to give a good view of Act One of the drama.

Helver wasn't sure how he was to make her acquaintance. Dogs were fond of him, and he had high hopes the pug would take a leap at his fawn trousers, which would require an apology from the owner. If that failed he could always fall into a fit of distraction and accidentally brush against her and be the maker of apologies himself. That they should pass without becoming firm friends never entered his head, nor hers, either. But none of the ruses were necessary. While he was still two steps away from her and edging closer to brush her shoulder (the dog was heading off in the wrong direction) Lady De Courcy stopped walking and said in delighted surprise, "Well, if it isn't Helver Trebourne!" The surprise was not quite genuine, for she had been looking through her own curtains for a week waiting for him to come to town.

"Good day, Ma'am," he said, lifting his hat with his one free hand and taking the last step to put him within touching distance of her. He hadn't the faintest idea who she might be; but he knew she was no local siren, so he said next, "I am surprised to see you in Tisbury, Ma'am. London, wasn't it, that we met?"

"Brighton, I believe, if memory serves me aright," she answered and wondered if it was possible he had forgotten her. For a whole week he had been a constant companion of Bertie, her late husband, and herself. But, then, he hadn't really been very sober for any part of that week, and what memories he had of the period might more likely center on a female named Audrey.

"Ah, yes, Brighton. Visiting in Tisbury, are you? I hope you mean to make a long stay."

"Very long. I live here now. Since Bertie's death, I am come here to rusticate."

"Bertie" rang no more bells than the fair charmer herself, but this was suppressed as a matter of course. "Bertie dead, is he? I am sorry to hear it." He wondered what degree of grief it would be proper for him to exhibit and contented himself with wiping away his smile.

"Yes, three years ago. And Willowdale was entailed on his brother, you know, so I now am a widow thrown out on the cruel world."

That Bertie's passing had made this vision of loveliness a widow was news good enough to make his grave expression difficult to maintain, but still he could put no name to the lively face. "The world cannot be cruel to one so beautiful," he said with a gracious bow.

"I'm sure everyone has been very kind. Your dear mother has been to call, and your Aunt Sara. Dear Egbert has been a pillar to me. But you have problems of your own, Helver, and I not offering a word of sympathy. I was so sorry to hear of your papa's death. I shall miss that dear man." She had never actually met the late Duke, but a corpse was in no position to say so, and she took him on as a surrogate father. "And how do you like being the Duke?"

The woman appeared to know all about him and his family, and he was becoming quite embarrassed at his inability to remember her. How did it come she had not been mentioned at home? He muttered some banalities about the death and his new position and then said, "Have you been here long?"

She observed his difficulty in recognizing her and decided to give him a hand. "Almost two years. When Lord De Courcy passed away — a hunting accident, you remember how horse-crazy dear Bertie was — I tried a while at the Dower House, but really it was impossible. In the wilds of Cornwall, you must know; and when I came to Tisbury I said to Aunt Abbott, my *chaperone*, she calls herself, 'This is where we shall settle down, Aunt,' and so we did. In that little house there on the corner — just a tiny little shelter for me to hide away and grow old in." A youthful smile accompanied this lugubrious suggestion.

"It is Tisbury's gain, Lady De Courcy," he smiled back, reinforcing her name by using it at once. "May I do myself the honour of calling on you one day?"

"We are always pleased to receive callers every morning," she told him and added to herself, "especially when they are eligible young dukes." "I go out very little and would be delighted to receive you. I have few callers since your dear papa is gone. Bring your mama with you. Do give my respects to the Duchess."

He bowed, replaced his curled beaver on his head and walked on, feeling much happier to be back. Milady continued her stroll but still forgot to unfurl her parasol, for her mind was full of schemes to entrap him. And little Billie Paul, only eight years old, who was the sole member of the community to have overheard their conversation, was passed from door to door to be given cookies and other unwonted treats and asked slyly what the pretty lady was saying to Helver. He was able to give only a garbled account, having centered his interest on the dog, but he was sure they were old friends, for the pretty lady was talking all about the Duchess and asking him to bring her to call.

The villagers' opinion of the morals of both Lady De Courcy and Helver Trebourne could hardly have been lower, but on the subject of manners both were held to be unexceptionable, the former for having snubbed them all and the latter for speaking and smiling to everyone whether he knew them or not. Therefore, it was not assumed by even the sternest matron that they had hove to for a ten-minute chat on no previous acquaintance. It had not been necessary for the pug to be unleashed, so Milady must have been sure of recognition. The next event to be watched for was the arrival of a crested carriage at Milady's door, and, if that happened, the spring's entertainment was secured.

Helver was certainly keenly interested in the young widow, but her knowing his family, far from standing in her favour, was a detriment. It was one thing to carry on with a rackety young widow and quite something else to go calling in state with his mama on a respectable lady, available for marriage. This second course was one he had no notion of pursuing. Lady De Courcy was beautiful, friendly and possibly even a real lady, but he strongly suspected that she was open for dalliance. There was invitation in those amorous dark eyes, and a clinging gown of the sort the lady wore was not chosen to please the women. He went to the bother of looking her up in Debrett's Baronetcy, and he saw her to be the relict of a fifty-seven-year-old minor baron and of no noble stock herself. He still couldn't recall one single detail of any friendship in Brighton and assumed that she had made it up. Claiming a friendship with his father gave him a good idea that she was a liar because the Duke had not been long alive while she was in Tisbury, and quite ill at that time. Next he must find out how strong was this friendship with his mother and aunt. She could hardly have claimed to be on terms with them if it were not at least partially so.

"Where are my peppermint drops?" his mother asked when they all met at dinner.

"It slipped my mind, Mama. I'm terribly sorry. I'll pick them up tomorrow."

Pained looks of resignation were exchanged by the Duchess and her sister. "Oh, that's all right, Helver. I know you are too busy to think of *me*," his mother replied. "I daresay I shan't close an eye this night with the tickle in my throat, but don't worry about it. I can always take some laudanum if I'm still awake at two o'clock or three o'clock."

"I'll go back to the village after dinner, Mama, and get them. Or you can send a footboy."

"Yes, I'd better send a boy, for I *would* like to have them." It was pretty clear that even a second trip brought no assurance she would do so, if Helver were the delivery boy.

"The man came to look at the roof," Egbert said. "Said the whole thing must be changed. It will cost you a pretty penny."

"That is nonsense," the Duchess declared. "Saymore would not have let it fall into decay. He always kept everything up. It is only a few slates, I daresay. When will he do it?"

"He is coming to see Helver," Egbert advised.

"Tell him to go ahead with it," Helver said with an impatient wave of the hand, for he wanted to get on with talking about the Baroness De Courcy. "I met a newcomer in the village today."

"He is coming to see you," Egbert repeated. "He mentioned something in the nature of hundreds of pounds. I could not tell him to do it."

"Yes, it must be done. We have to have a roof over our heads. About this lady in the village — Lady De Courcy is her name."

"You'd better see him, Helver," his mother continued with the conversation preferred by the elders. "We don't want a whole new roof if a few shingles are all that are required."

"Mama, you have said the whole top floor is awash. It can't be only a few shingles. The roof hasn't been worked on for as long as I can remember. Tell him to do it — do a good job. This Lady De Courcy, she claims acquaintance with you and Aunt Sara."

This claim finally got their attention. "With *me*? Why, she said she was a great friend of *yours*!"

"I think I met her once, at Brighton. Baron De Courcy's wife she was at that time. But were you not to call on her?"

"Call on her!" Sara gasped. "Your papa would have gone through the roof. He thought her common and forthcoming in the extreme. She used to wink and smile at him in church the first few Sundays she was here. Your dear papa was still dragging himself out to church in those days. I don't think he should have done it."

"I thought she mentioned you had been to call," Helver said.

"Is *that* what she's saying, the vixen," Lady Sara said in injured accents. "So that's how she interpreted it, to say we were *calling* on her. I knew just how it would be. I daresay she put the grease on the street herself to trip us."

"I shouldn't be quite so uncharitable as that in my view," Lady Saymore objected, wearing a pious expression. "It doesn't do to look for the worst in people, Sara, and she was quite a good Samaritan to us. Only, of course, she is a common little trollop."

Travers smiled at Helver at this charitable opinion, and he asked, "What happened, exactly?"

"Your mama and I were in the village," Sara enlightened him. "There was a spill of grease on the street in front of her house, that little house there on the corner she has taken and painted the door bright red and put a new knocker on it. Your mama slipped and fell. She didn't actually fall right down but skidded, you know, and wrenched her knee. Lady De Courcy sent out a servant to see if she could be of help, and as your mama was a little shaken, we went into her saloon to recover. She came and introduced herself, and gave us a glass of wine."

"It was very poor stuff. No lemon juice or nutmeg in it," his mother added.

"She was quite civil and said she knew you very well," Sara took up her narrative. "But when she all but got down on her knees to beg us to come to call, despite our not asking her to do so (and she did some pretty broad hinting, too) one could not but wonder if she is quite the thing. Well, the De Courcys, you know, are all fools, and the Baron might have married anyone. She was his second wife, she says. She has the look of an actress about her. Those gowns . . ."

"A stylish dresser," Egbert said, knowing he was voicing an unpopular opinion.

"They have no opinion of her in the village," Travers warned Helver. "She don't speak to any of the womenfolk but is on good enough terms with all the men. And for all she's a Baroness, they do say she's as clutch-fisted as may be. I can't make heads or tails of her. What would have brought her to a place like Tisbury if it's a match she's looking to make? But she goes up to London for the Season. Maybe she stays here to save her money to be able to afford it."

This came close to being the truth. Travers held a further suspicion that Tisbury had been chosen with Helver in mind, but in this she did her Ladyship an injustice. She had inherited a mortgage on the house; then, when the owner defaulted, she came into it and found it a useful place to wait for the Season.

Travers was too cagey to hint to Helver that he was the magnet drawing Milady here. If he took the idea she had scrambled all the way from Cornwall to see him, he might take into his head to favour her with a flirtation. Travers had been dreading the day he came home smiling, as he was today, and asking about De Courcy.

"She is not a family friend, then?" Helver confirmed, happy to hear it.

"If you call sitting in her living room for ten minutes to recover your breath friends, then we are friends," Sara said. "That is the extent of our acquaintance with her, and let me add, Helver, it as close as we wish the association to go. That house — she had it rigged out like a bordello."

"Are you much acquainted with the decor of bordellos?" Helver asked quizzingly.

Lady Sara never made a joke and never suspected anyone else of it. She answered in all seriousness, "No, *I* personally have never been in one, though I should like to see what they're like. But in the pictures in our illustrated copy of *Scheherezade* there are things similar to Lady De Courcy's saloon. We only saw her front saloon, of course. A great many cushions of rich materials on her sofa — satins and velvets. Strange globes on her candles, with crystal pendants hanging on them; but I think it was the use of purple and gold that gave the impression I speak of."

Helver formed a good idea of the garishness soon to greet his eyes when he called on Lady De Courcy, for what he had heard made the call eminently suitable in his view.

Travers alone at the table read the workings of his mind and undertook to give him a warning. "She's not the loose sort of a woman you might think to look at her. She don't carry on with the men but for a little smiling in public. No one ever says that of her, and you may be sure they'd say it if there was so much as a hint of a cause. She looks like a dasher — anyone might be fooled by her appearance — but in my mind it's marriage she has in her eye. Anyone who takes to courting her had better be thinking along those lines, or he might find himself in trouble."

Helver smiled meaningfully at his old friend and said, "Your caveat has been noted."

"Eh? What's that you say, Helver?" Sara asked.

"I said very likely Travers is right."

"Oh, yes, very likely. She's as sharp as a thorn, is Milady. That's what they call her in the village."

CHAPTER
SIX

Dame Durden did not happen to be in the village
during the meeting of Milady and Helver Trebourne;
but she arrived there not long afterwards to visit the
library, and Edith was with her. While Edith went
through the few shelves looking for *The Divine
Comedy*, the Dame was told that young Helver was
setting up a flirtation with the widow. It was no more
than she expected, but she did not mention the Duke
to Edith unless she felt it to be necessary. The less her
mind was occupied with him the better. Still she felt
that when Edith became even more restless and
irritable than usual he was the cause of it, and she
worried. She spoke a good deal of Dorion Thorne that
evening without receiving more than a nod or a sigh in
reply.

In the village Lady De Courcy had no reason to be
so reticent about her hopes for the young Duke. She
plumped up her purple and gold satin cushions and
waited for her knocker to pound. Her "Aunt Abbott,"
who was in truth no relative at all, but a friend from the
acting profession employed to give her countenance
and an air of respectability, sat with her. The chaperone
was a formidable big woman with a face like a man,

even including a few whiskers about the chin. She was outfitted all in black bombazine, and from her fingers a bit of knitting was suspended. It was one of her stage props and had not increased a fraction of an inch in all the years she had held it. She had worked out a bit of business which gave a very good appearance of real knitting, but the wool did not actually come in contact with the needles.

"Now if he comes, you're not to leave the room, Abbott," Blanche said. Lady De Courcy was born Agnes White and commonly called Whitey by her childhood associates. But on the day she went on the stage the name had been translated into French for purposes of elegance.

"I know my role, Blanche," the matron replied. Blanche was punctiliously "Lady De Courcy" or "Milady" in public, but in private no formality existed between these thespians.

"I doubt he'll come at night," Blanche said. "I most particularly invited him to come any *morning*." It was now evening of the day of their first meeting.

"It'll be a sign," Abbott decreed. "If he waits till morning, he's serious; and if he don't, he's up to no good."

"If he comes at night he'll soon learn he'd better be up to good or nothing. I don't mean to let him make a mockery of me before this whole damned village. I don't suppose the Duchess will come. He might bring Egbert. Egbert would be happy enough for an excuse to get his form inside my door. Maybe you should take a crack at Egbert, Abbott."

"Not with that watch dog of a Lady Sara guarding him. They say the Duke is a rare one. I think you're flying too high, Blanche. You'd best watch your step."

"It's only April. If nothing comes of this month, I'll go on up to London for the Season. I don't mean to let a duke go by without stirring a finger to nab him."

"He's a handsome rascal."

"Yes, more's the pity. If he were an ugly old coot like Bertie, my chances would be better. This one has as many girls as he wants for the asking, I make no doubt."

"I think you're wasting your energy; but, as we don't leave for a few weeks, it will be something to pass the time."

"If you'd seen the way he scooted across the street to meet me, you wouldn't be so sure. He's interested, but in *what*? I made it as clear as I could that I was respectable."

Their discussion was interrupted by a loud sound of the knocker. They looked at each other. "Damn!" Blanche said. "I *did* hope he'd come in the morning."

But when Helver was shown in, her pretty face bore no trace of resentment at his nocturnal visit. "Why, Helver, come so soon to bear me company. How sweet of you."

Helver's eyes flickered from the stunner to the trappings of her quasi-bordello, as he considered her saloon, and halted at the bale of bombazine occupying the chair by the grate.

"My aunt, Mrs Abbott," Blanche said. "This is the Duke of Saymore, Aunt. A good friend of Bertie's; and, of course, you know his mama, the Duchess."

The two said what was necessary, and Helver was given a seat beside Lady De Courcy on the gold sofa. "How is the Duchess?" Blanche asked, determined to keep a decorous tone to the proceedings.

"Well. That is, her throat is bothering her a little. I came to town to get her some peppermint drops and dropped by, as you were so kind as to ask me."

"So *that's* why you are paying an evening call! I did wonder as I mentioned quite specifically I am at home most mornings. But I am always happy to see Bertie's friends any time you are in the village," Blanche said. She wished to be both friendly and firm at the same time.

"My mornings, and also afternoons, are greatly occupied these days with all the work to do on the estate. It has had an absentee landlord for nearly a year and a half, as I was abroad when my father died."

Blanche digested this, and while she asked for a recital of his trip and got it she came to the hard decision that she must allow evening visits. It was asking for trouble, not what she wanted at all; but no visits she wanted even less, and there might be some truth in his claim of being busy. And the nights were endless to get through for that matter. What was the point in getting all dressed up with no one to see her but Abbott?

They chatted for half an hour, had a glass of wine and, at the end of that period, Helver began glancing at Aunt Abbott in a questioning manner. If the old bale of bombazine was to remain the whole time, he might as well leave. Blanche read and correctly interpreted his every glance and gesture. When he pulled out his timepiece, she said suddenly, "Oh, Aunt, did you remember to ask Cook to buy a goose for tomorrow?"

Abbott, more jealous of Blanche's virtue than the lady herself, replied firmly, "Yes, I did, Lady De Courcy."

"Dear Aunt, she never forgets a thing," Blanche said to Helver with an apologetic smile. "Would you care for some macaroons with your wine, Helver?"

He wanted a macaroon as much as he wanted a bout of measles, but, sensing that Abbott was to go for them, he declared there was nothing he preferred to a macaroon.

"Would you be so kind, Aunt?" Blanche asked, with a steely command in her eyes.

Abbott had no option but to go, but meant to be back within three minutes. Her short absence was enough for Helver to get right to the point.

"Does your aunt always sit with you in the evenings?" he asked.

"Why, Helver, you must know it wouldn't be at all the thing for me to entertain a male guest unchaperoned."

"You're not a deb," he pointed out, "but a married lady. Surely a widow may be deemed capable of entertaining whom she wishes without a doyenne."

"People *do* talk, you know, and I don't want them talking about me." This confirmed her uncertain standing within the realm of respectability. A lady born and bred need not be so jealous of her reputation.

"You never entertain a man without a chaperone, then?" he asked bluntly.

Blanche knew as surely as he was sitting on her gold settee that he would never occupy it again if she told him this was the case. "She often retires early," she compromised.

"How early?" he asked, not choosing, apparently, to waste a single minute in chaperoned activity.

Blanche was not willing to throw herself on his mercy so easily and equivocated. "Why, earlier some evenings than others. It depends on how tired she is."

"She appears to be unfatigued this evening. May I count on you to take her for a long walk tomorrow and send her to bed early?"

"I believe the stories one hears of you are true, Helver. I'm not sure I care to have you call on such terms as you outline."

He hunched his shoulders in complete indifference and arose to leave, the macaroons forgotten. He was an imposing figure, standing in her saloon in his well-cut jacket, with his black hair styled in the latest mode and his dark eyes running over her décolleté gown. And he was a duke. This was more important in the long run than the rest, but for that fraction of a moment it was more the man than the duke she regretted losing.

"Well?" he asked. There was not even the saving pretence of his being interested in anything but an affair. Her staunch resolve had been to permit nothing of the sort, but she wavered.

"If you care to come by tomorrow evening, we might discuss it."

68

"I'll be here at nine-thirty," he said. "Good evening, Lady De Courcy."

"You were used to call me Blanche," she reminded him.

"Is that your name?" he asked blandly. "Good evening, Blanche."

With a smile he was off; and, when Abbott returned with the macaroons within three minutes, Blanche was sitting alone, her chin in her hands.

"Had to send him packing already?" Abbott asked. "I told you how it would be. A gentleman who makes his first call in the evening is up to no good."

"Shut up, Abbott," Blanche said.

"Never mind, there will be London to look forward to. There's more than one fish in the sea."

"There aren't many as worth landing as this one. I rather fancy this particular fish."

"The one that got away is always the one a body particularly wanted."

"He hasn't got away yet. He returns tomorrow evening, and you will bear me company, as usual."

"If he don't throw me in the cellar and bolt the door. He looked as if he wanted to."

A soft laugh emitted from the divinely obscene lips of Milady, and the two women sat down to consume the macaroons and lay plans.

In the houses of the village the arrival and departure of the curricle — he hadn't driven his crested carriage — were noted, and it was a matter for deep consideration whether half an hour was long enough for the lecherous goings-on that they imagined to have been consummated.

The Duke of Saymore was on time for his meeting the next evening, and Aunt Abbott, as well as Lady De Courcy, was there to greet him. And there they both stayed. A half an hour might possibly have encompassed an abbreviated orgy, but a quarter of an hour clearly had not, and there was rampant speculation as to what had gone forth. It was feared by some that Milady was winning, and they would soon have the galling view of the old Duchess trotting into the red-doored domicile. Then two nights passed without any sign of the curricle, and Tisbury breathed a sigh of relief.

A chance meeting in the village on the third day after Helver's last visit rekindled his hopes of yet getting the delicious widow to himself.

"Aunt Abbott and I have been walking for *miles*," Blanche said with a provocative smile. "I daresay she will be dead tired by this evening."

"Does walking not tire you, Blanche?" he asked with a significant question in his voice.

"I never go to bed till all hours. I shall be up half the night. I'll just sit alone and read till one o'clock or two o'clock."

"Would you care for some company?" he asked promptly.

"How kind you are. That would be lovely."

"About ten o'clock?" he asked — an unseemly hour for a call and one that would tell the villagers only too surely the reason for it.

"Say nine-thirty," she countered.

70

He misconstrued this as a sign of eagerness on the lady's part and was there at nine-thirty on the dot with a garnet bracelet in his pocket, only to be met once again by the omnipresent Abbott, her whiskers bristling at Blanche's stunt. The angry look he directed at Blanche was sufficient for her to blush, and she suggested to Abbott that she was looking haggard. This and a few more hints went unheeded, and she finally had to stamp her little foot and command, "Go, I say, Abbott."

Abbott went but was back every five minutes with some foolish question or other so that Helver no sooner got his arm around Milady's waist than they were interrupted. He didn't get the opportunity to produce the garnet bracelet at all, which might very well have turned the trick. He left, but the visit had stretched to nearly an hour, and there was no doubt in the mind of the village that "that Helver Trebourne" had done it again. They were in no way displeased with their boy this time, much as they chided him behind his back. Their real fear was that the Duchess would take to calling on the bold hussy, and clearly this fear could be set aside.

There were a few more visits spread out over the next two weeks, but it had become clear to Blanche that she would get no more than the necklace and earrings to go with the bracelet; and as she knew to a penny what they were worth, she wrote off to London to hire a flat for the Season. Helver was angry with himself for having been made a May-game of. Really, he hardly even found Milady attractive. Was he becoming so discriminating, then, in his maturity, he wondered.

71

But before it was broken off — the lady considered it still possible of *some* gain before she left for the City — the news of the affair was ripping through the neighbourhood and soon came to the ears of his family.

"Helver Trebourne, you have been to see that woman!" his mother accused on the day after the second visit.

"You mean Lady De Courcy?" he asked nonchalantly. "Yes, I have called on her."

"We do not call on her," Sara reminded him.

"You will observe that I have not asked *you* to call on her," he pointed out.

"I should hope not, for an *evening* call, you know, has such a very odd appearance to it."

"I happened to be in the village and am rather busy during the daytime."

"Happened to be in the village two nights in a row! Gone there only to call on that vixen, and for no other reason," Sara charged angrily.

"But how is this? It is usually the lowness of my companions that irks you. I had thought a Baroness must be unexceptionable."

"Baroness, hah. Actress is more like it."

"You are quite out. She was married to Baron De Courcy, who was personally known to me. She is always chaperoned by a formidable lady twice my size, as well. I couldn't have my way with her if I tried."

"Such talk as this is not suitable for the dinner table, Helver," his mother decreed. "You did not talk so at table when your father was alive."

72

"I did not talk at all, for my father never gave me the chance. But it appears to have slipped your notice this is now *my* house, and I shall talk as I please at my own table. This particular subject was not of my choosing, however; and as it is no one's business but my own whom I choose to associate with, we shall not discuss it further."

There was little discussion of any sort after this snub; and, immediately the meal was over, Helver went to the stable and climbed into his curricle to go in search of amusement.

"Something must be done or that woman will marry Helver!" Lady Sara said to the Duchess after he had gone.

"What he needs is a wife," Egbert pointed out. Being a male, he could think of no finer wife for Helver than the widow, but he did not actually say it.

"Indeed, it is God's plan that man should marry," the Duchess told them. "It is high time Helver brought us home a bride."

"Yes, and it is not Milady he will bring us," Sara said firmly. "He must marry a real lady; someone we will not be ashamed to be related to, who will not go turning the Blue Saloon into a bordello."

"Now who shall he marry, Dora?" Sara asked her sister.

"Eddie Durden is a nice girl," Travers mentioned.

"Yes, she is a nice little thing," Sara said consideringly, "but Dame Durden wouldn't hear of it. She calls us mongrels. Besides, Helver might look higher than an armiger's daughter for a wife."

"Squire Durden was never in the army," Egbert objected at once.

"Dame Durden was telling us at the Historical Society meeting that an armiger is someone who is entitled to a coat of arms. Her husband was an armiger, for what it's worth; but still they are not titled, for all their airs, and a man in Helver's position ought to align himself with one of the other noble families. Hasn't Lord Carlton an unmarried daughter, Dora?" Sara asked.

Lord Carlton's estate was only twenty-five miles away and the family well known to the Trebournes, but still Dora could not quite recall whether it was a son or daughter Carlton had living at home.

"It's a daughter, all right," Travers told them. "As near to a moonling as may be, but a pretty little thing."

"Well, there you are then," Sara said at once. Imbecility was no bar to eligibility; so long as the girl was pretty Helver would like her. "Write Lord Carlton a note, Dora, and invite the girl — now what is her name?"

"Anne," Travers told them.

"Ask them to send Lady Anne to us for a few weeks, and we'll see if Helver don't marry her."

"An excellent idea. Write to her, Travers, and I'll sign my name," the Duchess declared, well satisfied with this cunning way of managing matters.

"All right," Travers agreed, shaking her head at their simple scheme. As though Helver would be caught by a witless girl of sixteen years!

74

The letter was written that same night and posted in the morning. It was received with joy in the Carlton household, where hopes of getting Annie settled favourably did not run high due to her feebleness of mind. The invitation was considered as leading possibly to a match; and though Helver was called "a bit of a high flyer" by the Earl when he talked the matter over with his countess, he was by no means to be turned off for such a paltry consideration. Lady Anne was put into a carriage and sent off the very next day, and arrived before nightfall. Helver talked to her, or rather at her (she seldom spoke), for fifteen minutes after the tea tray was brought in before excusing himself and reverting to less elevated but more articulate associates for the remainder of the evening.

CHAPTER
SEVEN

It had been becoming increasingly clear to Dame Durden for some few days that Edith was out of spirits. She mooned about the house in a trance, and, as this fit of melancholy had arrived hard on Helver Trebourne's heels, she thought she knew the cause of it. She had heard from Sally that Helver had made a good long stay on his visit, and, if that ninny of an Edith was not falling in love with him, it was more than she knew. She revised her opinion of mentioning him, for it was clearly her duty to let her daughter know what he was up to.

"I hear Helver is up to his old tricks," she said one fine afternoon.

"What has he done now, Mama?" Edith asked with a sinking heart.

"He is traipsing after that Lady De Courcy, from what I hear in the village."

"Oh dear!" Edith said. She took as active an interest in Milady's conduct as everyone else, but, living out of the village, she was not aware of the watching through the curtains that went on there. She had been thinking so much of Helver and herself that it had never even occurred to her that he would be entertaining himself in that direction; but once the idea was presented to her, she felt it to have been inevitable. She had never so much as said hello to Milady, and, as she had no familiarity with city fashions, she knew neither that the widow was a vulgar trollop nor dressed like a strumpet. She knew only that she was a beautiful, titled lady that every man in Tisbury loved and that Helver might very well marry.

"It is only what everyone expected, I'm sure," the Dame went on. "The romance must be catching fire. That fool of a Dora has brought in Carlton's simple-minded daughter as a counterattack. They'll try to push that moonling on him, when they should be looking about for a *decent* match for him. Not that any decent woman would have him."

"Do you not think he will marry Lady De Courcy?" Edith asked.

"My dear, she is not the sort of a woman a man *marries*. I don't doubt for a moment he is leading her on, promising marriage perhaps; but you may be sure he won't offer his title to a rackety widow without a sou to her name."

"He wouldn't do that, Mama. If he has said he will marry her, he will."

"I haven't actually heard that he said anything of the sort. It cannot be the case that he has marriage in mind, for the Duchess has not been next or nigh the woman. No, she is his latest flirt, but sly as a fox; and she may wangle an offer yet. I must say, I am glad he never came back here. We don't want him hanging around, giving you a bad name."

Edith couldn't find the heart to agree with this. She had hoped to see him come again; but, of course, it would be a beautiful, worldly lady such as the Baroness he would be interested in.

"It's a fine day, Edith. Why don't you go and pick us some berries? The bushes where our land meets Saymore's have some good elderberries. I'll put up my cordial this week."

"All right, Mama."

"Take Sally with you," the Dame added.

Sally did not usually go to pick berries with Edith, and she suspected the servant was being sent on this occasion in case she should happen to run into Helver. For that same reason she was eager to go alone and did so, making the excuse to Sally that the best bushes were a mile away, and she could ride faster than walk, as they must if Sally came along. She did not bother explaining this change of plans to her mother, however.

She picked berries for an hour, filling her container while she looked occasionally across the meadow for a sign of Helver's bay mount. It was four o'clock, and she was about to go home when she spotted him riding past several feet away. He didn't see her and she didn't call him, as she did not like to act directly against her mother's wishes. That much conscience remained to her. She would not throw herself in his way. She just stood and watched how well he sat his mount, how gracefully they moved together, how in tune with nature. Then his horse spotted hers, tethered to a tree, and whinnied, calling Helver's attention to her. He immediately reined in and turned in her direction, smiling and waving.

"Hello, Eddie. Is the *femme fatale* sunk to picking gooseberries?" he joked.

"No, elderberries for Mama's cordial; and you should have yours picked, too. Look at them all going to waste." She pointed to his land, where the berries drooped in the sun.

"Help yourself if you wish. Mama doesn't make cordial, thank God! Has the Dame stuck by her decision not to have the May Day party?" He got down from his mount and pulled a few berries from the bush to toss into her basket.

"Yes. She lacks a queen. No girl in her right mind would do it."

It darted into Helver's head that Lady Anne was well qualified on that score, but, with some new sense of decorum, he didn't say it. "That's too bad. By the way, we have a visitor at the Hall. Lady Anne, Carlton's daughter, is staying with us. Do you think I might bring her to call on you one day?"

Helver had observed Eddie's growing up, and, while he hadn't liked it a bit at first, he had been impressed enough that he thought of her from time to time and had been wondering if he should call again. The Dame didn't like him, he knew, but Lady Anne formed a good excuse; and it would also pacify the relatives who were always pinching at him to be nice to the visitor.

"I guess it would be all right if she came with you," Edith said with a memory of her mother's delight that he wasn't hanging around the Court.

This answer revealed to Helver just what he thought, that the Dame disliked him. "Did she dislike my coming the other day?"

"Oh, no, she said it was very civil."

"But it would be better if I not come again?" he asked.

"You know Mama," she laughed deprecatingly.

"And worse, Mama knows *me*! What a trial it is, being always suspected of villainy."

"And you innocent as a newborn tiger!"

"And *you* sharp-tongued as an old cat all of a sudden. What's gotten into you? You didn't used to pester me whatever about the others."

"You didn't used to dangle after fast widows in those days."

"Yes, I did. Can you forget my passion for Widow Malone? But you refer, I collect, to the Widow De Courcy?" He looked closely at her as he asked this. "Who has been busy running to you with tales of my doings? I suppose it is all over the village. I would have thought young ladies of tender years would be spared."

"Oh, no, we are the very ones who are particularly warned away from those of your ilk."

She gave him a saucy smile, but there was no smile in return. He looked quite angry. "Bluebeard and Henry VIII and the Duke of Saymore, you mean?"

"Well, I *think* those two gentlemen married their ladies, didn't they? Whereas you, of course, don't bother."

"I just have my way with them, you mean?" he asked in a significant voice. Edith's back was to a tree and, advancing towards her, Helver leaned his arms on the tree, with her caught in their circle. His head loomed over hers, and his eyes held a wicked gleam. "Aren't you afraid of me, Eddie? All alone here with miles and miles of nobody. Old Bluebeard Trebourne, you know — God only knows what I might do to you."

She looked surprised for an instant, then burst into delighted laughter. "You're trying to scare me, Helver Trebourne! As if I'd be afraid of you."

"What, you don't believe the stories of my monumental debauchery?" he asked, stepping back and lowering his arms. "There's a facer for me," he answered, laughing. "I made sure I had you trembling in your boots, as you were when I chased you with that green snake we found by the creek."

"You didn't really put it down my neck when you caught me."

"No, and didn't really drown you in the creek, or push you out of the tree either. A model of propriety when you take a look at my record. I did everything but beat you. In fact, didn't I box your ears once?"

"No, you didn't!"

"I did, though. Remember when my cousin Larry came that summer and pelted around with us? You took quite a shine to him. You must remember."

"I remember Larry. He used to bring me candy."

"So he did, and would never give me a bit — you, either. We were squabbling over something or other, and you took Larry's side. I gave you a sharp box on the ear. You cried buckets."

"I think I do remember it now. And Larry beat you."

"He tried to, and you lit into him like a termagant. The two of us sent him home with his cork drawn. Lord, how did I remember that? It must have been ten years ago, at least. I wonder why you kept coming here to run around with me. A glutton for punishment, that's what you were. Do you still ride here as you used to?"

"Yes, all the time."

"We'll likely be meeting often, then. I come home this way from my jaunts with Forringer. Usually at about this time."

"I'm usually here earlier."

"How much earlier?"

"Around three o'clock usually," she said, her eyes sparkling, for she sensed the conversation was not so casual as it sounded and sensed, too, that she was doing something her mama would strongly disapprove of.

"Three o'clock. I expect I'll be coming home a little earlier since Lady Anne is with us. Must do the pretty, you know."

"Yes. Well, my basket is full. I'd best be getting home."

"Yes. Eddie — I'll bring Lady Anne to see you tomorrow instead of meeting you here."

It was out in the open now. They were to meet in the meadow by prearrangement, and she felt a wild and sinful pleasure in it. She thought it pleased Helver, too. Making formal calls was too tame for him. She was correct in her surmise that it pleased him. It did, but he hardly knew why. His romantic fancies at the time were centered around Milady. He helped her onto her

82

mount, and stood looking after her as she rode away. She looked back over her shoulder and waved at him. The only thought in his mind was that she was going to drop her berries if she didn't look sharp about her.

At Saymore Hall the relatives, rather than finding it unusual Helver should take Lady Anne to visit an eligible lady twice as attractive as herself, thought it a wonderful idea.

"If the two girls hit it off, it will get Lady Anne out of our hair," Sara said. "The Dame won't send Eddie here, but she'll ask Anne to the Court likely."

It was possible for mongrels to call at the Court; otherwise the ladies would have been quite alone. In fact, the purebred Durdens even visited mongrel homes when it was perfectly clear the visit was bestowing an honour. It was only when worldly wealth and titles gave the mongrels the idea they were equals (there was no such a thing as a better) that they declined to visit. This cut them off from close intimacy with all persons who should have formed their natural circle of friends; but it maintained their dignity and, in the Dame's view, superiority.

Helver brought Lady Anne to call, and the simple child sat in a corner looking at Edith's old picture books and eating sugar plums while the grown-ups conversed. It was not a fruitful visit. With a duke and an earl's daughter under her roof, Dame Durden unbent enough to sit and talk and take tea with them, so that conversation was stilted and unnatural. Helver expressed his regret that the May Day revels were not to be held, which caused the Dame to look at Lady

Anne with a new interest; but May was already so close to being on them that there was no time for the requisite preparations.

He next made the unfortunate *faux pas* of enquiring whether she had made her elderberries into cordial yet. This was possible of an innocent interpretation. Helver knew she annually made it, but a certain guilty start in her daughter's eyes made her wonder. She had found out Sally had not accompanied Edith to the meadow, and as soon as the noble visitors had left, she put her suspicions to Edith.

"Did you meet Helver when you were out picking berries?"

"Yes, he happened to go by, Mama. He stopped for a minute." Edith blushed up to her eyes with shame and guilt, causing her mother a great deal of not unnatural worry.

"Odd you didn't mention it."

"I forgot," Edith said. She was a wretched liar.

"Have you been meeting him regularly, Edith?"

"No — no, indeed, I have not, Mama!" This at least had the ring of truth.

"It was just the one accidental meeting, then?"

"Yes. That is — I met him one other time, by accident."

"You find the meadow a felicitous place for *accidental* meetings, I see. I'll have no more of this, Edith. I'm disappointed in you. You know what Helver Trebourne is. An unprincipled rake. The whole village talking about his chasing after that De Courcy creature, and *you* already turning deceptive the minute he is back. He means to do you no good. If he were interested in anything but mischief, he wouldn't be meeting you there. He'd come to your door like a gentleman."

"But you said you didn't want him coming here!"

"I don't. But if he were interested in marriage — well, he isn't, so there's no point in talking about it. All that will happen is that you'll get a fast reputation that will give Doctor Thorne a disgust of you."

Edith stared. Was it *possible* her mother would actually permit her to marry Helver if he asked? Edith didn't ask. How could she, when Helver had never said a word about marriage or anything of the sort? And the Dame couldn't have answered the question if she had asked. He was a mongrel, but, from having lived out her entire life in the shadow of the Hall, some awareness of its importance had invaded the secret recesses of her mind. No denying it would be fine to have a Durden as next Duchess of Saymore. Why shouldn't the *real* aristocracy take its place in Society? This rationalization was knocking at her mind, begging entry, and who is to say whether it might not eventually succeed; but secret meetings in fields were something else again.

"So you are not to go near that east pasture again, Edith."

And just yesterday Edith had as well as told Helver she would see him there and that he shouldn't call at the Court. She frowned to see how her plans were all going awry; but it was, of course, impossible to confess to Mama the depth of depravity to which she had allowed herself to sink. "Well?" her mother asked sharply.

"All right, Mama." Edith knew she had done wrong to agree to meet him. Likely Mama was right, and she would only end up ruined if she went ahead and did so. She recalled the snickers behind the Widow Malone's back, and, as he was apparently quite openly seeing Lady De Courcy, no good could come of the meetings. She resolved to push Helver Trebourne out of her mind and reform herself, then promptly went to her room and remembered every word and look that had passed between them since his return.

For two days she dragged around the house like a bruised herb, and for two days Helver waited in the meadow from three o'clock to three-thirty, wondering why she didn't come. That sheer fickleness was at the bottom of it never occurred to him. She *often* came, she said, but not every day. The Dame was keeping her busy. He was disappointed and, on the third day, rather angry. On the fourth day he didn't bother going home by the meadow; he purposely went a mile out of his way to go home by the spinney. Unlike Edith, he didn't have all day to consider the matter. He was extremely busy, well into the building project along the river and taking a keen interest in the brick homes going up. Forringer, too, was deeply involved in this; and with both so busy, it was necessary to hire an assistant bailiff to tend to the more routine chores. The appointment of this man caused a new ripple of gossip.

"Who will you have for the post, then?" Forringer asked the Duke.

"The men are better known to you than to me. Who's the best man for the job?"

"There's Joe Sparks — a bit brighter than most and a good worker."

"Joe Sparks from the west quarter? I don't remember that he was ever good for more than riding like a wild man and chasing the petticoats. An old crony of my own."

"Aye, well one of the petticoats has caught him, over a year ago, and made a man of him. Young Bessie Moog. They've one babe in the nursery and another on the way. He's settled down to a good worker."

"Oh, a family man. Married Bessie Moog, eh? She was a pretty little wench."

"She still is."

"Very well, let's give Joe a try."

With his new status as assistant bailiff and his growing family, Joe approached Helver about acquiring one of the new brick homes. It was a little larger and fancier than some of the others. Joe was ambitious, hard-working and clever. Helver meant to hold on to him; and to achieve this he let Joe add a bedroom and a few items of outside ornament. He stopped occasionally at Joe's present cottage on matters of business, and it was soon circulating that the young Duke had taken a shine to Bessie Sparks and seen fit to make her man a bailey and give them a new house.

Dame Durden went more often than usual to the village these days, taking her daughter with her as she didn't dare leave her alone; and they heard all details of the appointment. Edith's shoulders drooped even lower than usual. Her mouth formed into its sad line, but all the same she listened with interest to the gossip. The Dame felt action was called for before she lost her looks entirely, and the action taken was to issue an invitation to Doctor Thorne to spend a few days at the Court.

CHAPTER
EIGHT

Doctor Thorne came to Durden Court with the greatest goodwill in the world to make himself agreeable to Edith and her mama and to cast himself a little in the Duke of Saymore's way if it should be possible, with an eye to being appointed Vicar of Tisbury. He was tall and thin, with a face not unhandsome — rather pale from being so often buried in his books but with bright, intelligent eyes. He took Edith to the village in her mama's carriage, rode with her in areas other than the east meadow, for he had been informed of the danger lurking in that quarter, and read to them in the evenings. It was diverting to have some company other than Mama and the servants to talk to, and Doctor Thorne was a good talker. As a man of the church, he tended to discuss religious matters a little more than was entertaining to laymen, and to discuss them, too, in an elevated style not always comprehensible to his audience. But Edith knew she was not a clever girl and tried to learn from him. He was a kind and patient teacher, explaining to her matters in which she tried to become interested.

Edith didn't realize it, but Dorion Thorne was making love to her. That he chose to do it by sermons and theological talk was perhaps a little unusual, but for him it was as good a way as any other. Edith liked him best in the pulpit. After a few days of roundabout romancing in the general duties of a Christian, Dorion felt it was time to bring the matter to a head. The Dame had conveniently excused herself to give him the opportunity, and the two sat in the main saloon discussing those attributes that constituted a good, useful life.

Dorion's path was cut out for him: he was to be a good shepherd as soon as he could find a fold in need of one; but Edith realized as she listened that her life was of no use to anyone. There was some imputation of selfishness on her part in the discussion; Dorion mentioned subtly her advantages in birth, breeding and worldly goods and asked, in effect, what are you doing to repay the Lord for all this. All she was doing was to moon around after a rake; and, while she didn't say so, she knew it and felt it was not enough. By minute, shifting degrees the Doctor gave her to understand that her real task in life, as a woman, was to align herself with some man with a mission. It was not till that instant that Edith tumbled to his intentions. He was the man and his the mission with which she was being asked to align herself.

"In short, Miss Durden, I am asking you to be my wife."

The first ridiculous thought to flit into her head was that there was no "in short" about it. It had taken him an hour. She looked at him, half flattered and half horrified. She no more wanted to marry him than she

90

wanted to marry the Archbishop of Canterbury; yet she respected him, knew him for a good, worthy man. She could not offend him.

"I cannot think I would be the proper wife for you, Dorion," she said, blushing.

"You must allow *me* to be the best judge of that," he answered playfully, assuming as a matter of course that it was only her awareness of her own inadequacies that led her to object. "I realize that in marrying a *young* girl I would need to give you some help in coming to understand your duties. I am willing, more than willing, to give you the guidance you will require. Indeed, it will be one of my chief pleasures to do so," he added, as a sop to romance.

"But I am not at all accustomed to — to dealing with many people, so retired a life as Mama and I lead here."

"They will be only simple people you have to deal with. Dame Durden's daughter must have many qualities, good qualities, she would be willing to share with the less fortunate."

Edith had had a Christian upbringing. Dorion was right; she should settle down and accomplish something with her life. Yet she was so far from wanting to accomplish what he outlined that she still prevaricated. "I must have time to think about it," she said.

This was not the reply he wanted or expected; but this was the girl he had chosen, and he was patient. "Certainly you must. Marriage is too serious a matter to fly into without consideration. I think when you have slept on it, you will see I am right. You must not fear you cannot handle the work, Edith. It is always better to take on a job in which there is room to grow, to let your talents expand and reach that fulfillment that is within you. You know well enough that I was for some few years studying the law; but after weighty consideration, I saw that a man's greatest achievement was not to be gained in such a paltry line of work. The greatest work a man can do, or a woman, either, is God's work and so I switched my studies to the church. I have never regretted it, and neither will you, if you will join me. Together we will bring God's word to that small corner of England where we are stationed. Our abilities, such as they are, will be put at His disposal. Can anyone ask more?"

With this ardent and unromantic speech he sought to win her. Not a word of love or affection. He spoke of marriage as a job, a piece of work to be done. She could not like it, yet she could admire it. It was always so with her. And after all his efforts, when she went to bed, she wondered if Helver knew Dorion was at the Court and if he was jealous. Really, she was not a worthy wife for Doctor Thorne, she thought, when she realized what she was doing.

It was while Doctor Thorne was visiting the Court that the spring assembly in Tisbury occurred, and Edith and the Dame were to be escorted to it by him. Doctor Thorne was not so singlemindedly religious that he failed to take in any party that offered. The Dame had a new peacock blue gown welded together, made up of the stiffest brocade ever seen anywhere. It fairly creaked and rattled when she walked, sounding like a loose tin roof in a violent storm. Edith was given a white crepe gown with green trim. She would have preferred pink or blue trim, but white and green were the Tudor colours, and there were many white and green features in the Durden residence — curtains, table covers, bed throws. Her sole adornment was a small enamelled brooch on which the Durden coat of arms was cast. Edith had not seen Helver for a week and he had seen no lady in a romantic way except Lady De Courcy. He considered that affair to be over; but still she was casting out lures, and the fish, she thought, had not yet absolutely got away.

There were elaborate preparations for the assembly in all the homes surrounding Tisbury. In the little residence across from the apothecary shop, the red door was frequently opened to admit a delivery boy, for the important decision had been taken that Milady and her chaperone should honour the local assembly with their presence. This would be a first, for such lowly pleasures, while they would have been greatly enjoyed, were disdained by the Peeress. She had heard rumours that the Duke of Saymore would attend, however, and so she was to go. Her last few meetings with him had been in the nature of wrestling matches, interrupted by Abbott before any points were scored. She wished to give him an opportunity to see and admire her without fear of being molested. She would be charming and flirtatious, and, if the Duchess attended, dignified into the bargain. All her histrionic abilities would be sorely tried, but she was not out of practice.

She laboured long over a suitable costume for the night's performance — something provocative enough to appeal to Helver, but not so *outrée* as to outrage his mother; and that it must turn all the ladies green with envy was a matter of course. She picked through the wardrobe she had been accumulating for the coming Season (which might or might not be attended in London) and selected a dashing emerald green gown to be set off by a necklace of diamonds that still held quite a few of the original stones, every second one having been prized out and sold to finance her Seasons in the City. With her titian hair dressed into an elaborate coiffure, she was off to wound the hearts of the people of Tisbury.

At the Hall, the Duchess had heard of the assembly but had no notion of attending it. When it was pointed out by Travers that Lady Anne might enjoy it, and Helver would certainly be going, pressure was brought to bear on Lady Sara and Egbert to accompany them.

"For he'll dump Lady Anne at the door and be chasing after all the girls, you know," the Duchess explained to her sister. "It would look bad if word got back to Carlton that Lady Anne was treated so." Such word was not likely to get back to the Earl by Lady Anne's own lips, but still, better not to take the chance.

When the crucial evening arrived, Helver stunned them all by announcing he had no thought of attending the dance. He had, indeed, the desire to do so; but, as he had observed no period of mourning for his deceased father at the proper time, he felt he ought to be doing it now.

"We've told Lady Anne you mean to take her," Sara told him. "See, she is all dressed for it."

Lady Anne sat on the sofa, looking very pretty in a white gown with blue ribbons while she rolled a blond curl around a finger in a mindless fashion. As the truth percolated through to her that she was to miss the dance, two large tears oozed out of her eyes and down her cheeks.

"Lady Anne is young to be going to dances," Helver objected. "Why, she's only a child, and I wager she can't dance, either."

The question was put to her by the Duchess, but she didn't answer.

"You don't dance, do you, Annie?" Helver asked, going over to sit by her side and speaking to her in a gentle tone.

"Yes," she said, looking at him with those injured, wet eyes.

"Do you want to go to this assembly?"

"Yes," she said again.

"What should I do, Travers?" Helver asked.

"I see no harm in going. We've given up mourning long ago."

"Very well, I'll take you," he said to Lady Anne, and she smiled a beatific smile at him.

"Mind you stand up with her, too," Sara cautioned. "And if that De Courcy creature is there, Helver, don't go making a cake of yourself by dancing at her petticoats all night."

"She doesn't go to the local dances," Travers said. There was such a thing as pushing Helver too far. That he must spend half the night looking after the little moonling was bad enough without telling him he must not dance with the most dashing lady in the room if she happened to be there. "Oh, Helver, if Edith Durden is there you might ask her to tell the Dame I found a very interesting book in the library about the Tudors. I'll send it over to her." This was done only to ensure that Helver seek out Edith. She felt he would do so, but if Milady attended, as she half feared she would, there was no counting on it. "It's a very good book. Be sure you tell her."

"I'll tell her," he said.

There were many points to ponder in the matter of strategy for the assembly. Lady De Courcy, having condescended to attend, was desirous of standing up for the opening minuet with the Duke. Her title led her to believe she would do so, but there was Lord Carlton's daughter visiting at the Hall. There were no secrets in the village. Lady Anne's presence at the Hall, the reason for it and its chances of failure had been talked over a dozen times. Might he not stand up with Lady Anne first? To be his second partner was not what Blanche wanted; and, to avoid this possibility, she would make a late entry. She was very fond of late entries in any case, the more dramatic the better. Let him have his duty dance with the moonling and he would be more than ready for a more worldly partner. The villagers could not then say he had neglected to stand up with her first.

Tisbury looked forward to this assembly with an eagerness unequalled since Helver had been dangling after the Widow Malone. It was but a dull affair last year, with him who should have been the chief source of interest not attending. That he would think of missing an assembly only because his father had died eighteen months ago was a streak of propriety not even considered. Oh, Helver Trebourne would be there all right; and, if the wise knew anything, Milady would come down off her high horse and be there, too. It was a disappointment that she did not appear before the first minuet. Some fears that she had changed her mind flared up, despite her having had Minnie Sproule in to do her hair and bought new silk stockings at the drapery shop. They had all been looking forward to smirking at her when Helver stood up first with Lord Carlton's daughter and were full of curiosity to see if she would honour Mr Hartman, the millionaire merchant. It was to be discovered, too, if she would unbend enough to stand up with anyone else but the two of them. Otherwise she would have a pretty flat night of it, for, if she thought to keep Helver to herself, she was out. He'd dance with every farmer's daughter and merchant's daughter that had a dimple or a trim waist.

They were kept pretty busy, however, seeing that their own sons and daughters were matched to their advantage and observing that that knock-in-the-cradle of a Lady Anne never opened her mouth and that Helver talked to her without interruption. Now would you have believed it, the little ninny could dance like a fairy. What the old Duchess had in her head to think to make a match there was beyond imagining but certainly not beyond prolonged gossip. It did not go undetected that Dame Durden had Doctor Thorne visiting, and it was considered an honour for this unemployed cleric to come amongst them. It was beginning to be talked up that he would get the Tisbury living and Dame Durden's daughter get the minister. This match had the wholehearted approval of the village. It was considered little short of inevitable that these two Saxons merge their blood, and it was not so grand a match for Edith that they were incited to jealousy.

Milady was a director and innovator as well as an actress. It was to be determined by having a footboy peeking in the windows of the assembly hall when the minuet was nearly over, at which time he was to dash back to Milady's residence and alert her to set out for the dance. She had decided to walk, not because the hall was only a short walk away, but so that she could drive home with the Duke of Saymore if all went according to plans. The closing bows of the minuet were regarded through the window, the footboy ran to deliver the news and Lady De Courcy and Abbott were soon entering the hall, their sharp eyes darting about to discover in which direction they should proceed.

Luck was with Lady De Courcy. Sir Egbert and Lady Sara sat at the edge of the floor waiting to receive Lady Anne back into their guardianship, and, as Milady strolled towards him, Egbert arose to scrape a leg. Sara would give him the very devil for it, but he never passed her in the village without a five-minutes flirtation, and he had no thought of eliminating this main pleasure from his existence because of Sara's crabbing. It was then necessary for Sara to shake two of Milady's fingers and say how do you do, in a pinched tone. All this happy welcome encouraged Milady to present Aunt Abbott to the nobility, and by then Helver was coming up to them with Lady Anne mute but smiling at his side. She danced so well Helver had even decided to stand up with her again for a country dance.

Blanche had the exquisite pleasure of being asked for the first dance it was physically possible for her to have with Helver; and though it was not a waltz, which would have capped her pleasure in getting him all to herself, it was a triumph nevertheless. She glanced to neither left nor right to gloat at Tisbury, but her heart was full, and the citizens were bilious to see her so elevated and clever.

"You haven't been to call on me for some time, Helver," she pouted with her infamous lips. "I am getting lonely."

"It seems to me you never lacked for company, Blanche. Quite the contrary."

"Oh, Aunt Abbott! She is no company."

"She accounts for the lack of it."

"Is the dear Duchess not here?" she asked, to steer the course back to calm waters.

"No, the dear Duchess doesn't care for assemblies. I had heard you didn't, either. It is an unlooked-for pleasure to find you here."

"Then it wasn't to stand up with *me* that you came?" she teased, laughing. "Dear me, what a leveller. Little Lady Anne is a treasure, is she not?" she asked next.

She was too shrewd to say a word against a sister peeress.

"Very pretty."

"A cut above the others here, the common people, I mean. We ought really not to associate with them — the Bixbys, the Mallens, the Durdens and so on."

The last name brought a sneer to Helver's lips. "The Durdens are likely the oldest and best-bred people in the room."

"So one hears. The Dame is a regular old quiz, is she not? How I laugh to see her stride through the village in those creaking old gowns and with that metal bag on her hair, as though she were doing Tisbury an honour."

"She is a bit of an eccentric," he admitted, having no particular fondness for the Dame.

"And her daughter setting up to be another. Only look at the odd gown she is wearing, cut to her neck and not a bit of jewelry but that funny looking old brooch with not a gem in it, and they letting on to have some money."

"It is not every woman who appears to advantage in dashing gowns and diamonds, Blanche. They suit you very well, but not a young girl."

"Well, I am not quite *old* yet, Helver. But Miss Durden is to be a minister's wife, of course, and such modesty becomes her in that circumstance."

"Who says she is to be Thorne's wife?" he asked sharply.

"Everyone. It is no secret the Dame asked him to the Court to bring him up to scratch."

"I hadn't heard he was visiting at Durden Court."

"Oh, lud, he's been there all week. I am sure he is there as much to pester you for the Tisbury living as anything else. The two of them are always jauntering through the village together. It is as well as settled. It's only the lack of a living that is preventing it. And you are to remove that stumbling block. It is time you appointed a vicar for the parish church."

"I won't be appointing that popinjay!"

"*Noblesse oblige*, Your Grace," she laughed. "It is expected you will. Why, the good doctor as well as told me that now you are home the appointment will be made. He used to dangle after *me*, you know, when first I came here, but I showed him the door fast enough when I saw what he was up to. Not a sou to his name; and, as to his fine old blood, he may keep it, or let it mingle with the Durdens'. There is not a title in his whole family either, or even a knight or a baronet. He would like well enough to give himself a leg up the ecclesiastical ladder by marrying a title, but he shan't marry *mine*."

"I am quite sure you do yourself an injustice, Blanche. I can't think it was just the title he was after but very likely the flesh and blood, as well."

"He liked the *flesh* well enough, whatever about the blood," she replied with a meaningful, taunting smile. "He isn't quite as full of starch as he lets on. Well, I hope he is happy with his starchy little Tudor. I wish him joy of her."

Helver took her boast with a grain of salt. He didn't believe for a minute that Thorne had ever looked twice at this hussy with any other view than disgust, or possibly redeeming her soul. The flirtation proceeded poorly; and even a hint that Abbott was always fagged to death after an assembly, whereas Lady De Courcy had the greatest trouble in the world getting to sleep, brought no offer to join her in her sleepless vigil. Helver was seriously alarmed to hear Eddie was on the verge of becoming engaged. She had mentioned Thorne to him as her most ardent suitor, but he had seen no real evidence of her caring for him. Looking at the pair of them now, he saw that Thorne was looking at her with the jealous eyes of a lover, and he felt angry. This, then, was why Eddie had not been to meet him, as she had half promised to do. Lady De Courcy had mocked Eddie's gown, but, to Helver, used to her quaint way of dressing, she looked very pretty. She had a well-shaped head, and the manner in which she wore her hair in a bun at the back lent her a touch of maturity, even elegance.

Thorne bent down to say something to her, and she looked up at him and smiled. What he said, in fact, was that the Duke of Saymore was looking at them, and, if he came that way, she might just mention that he was staying with them. Thorne was rather worried that his visit was reaching an end, with neither a position nor a wife having yet come into his hands.

CHAPTER
NINE

With Helver not coming to the Court and the meetings in the meadow cancelled, Edith was very eager for a sight of him. She knew the assembly would afford the opportunity and would afford, as well, her only possible chance of making Helver jealous with her suitor. But when the assembly finally came, the jealousy, she feared, was all allotted to herself. Of Lady Anne she could not be jealous, but to see Helver stand up with Milady did cause her a sharp sting and to see Milady in converse with Lady Sara and Egbert gave the whole affair a respectable colouring that she sadly mistrusted. Mama was wrong, and he planned to marry Lady De Courcy. Edith saw no flaw in her rival's ensemble, nor did she think Helver would do so. Her beautiful red hair looked so very elegant, all done in swirls, and the diamonds and bare shoulders had just the look of glamour and sophistication that must appeal to Helver after his tours to Spain and Italy. Dorion may mutter "vulgar" and "gaudy" as often as he liked, in common with other ladies in the room, but Edith secretly thought Milady the most fascinating lady ever to have come to Tisbury.

Edith had no hopes of getting the second dance with Helver after the redheaded siren entered the room, but she was still hoping to be the third one he stood up with and was keeping a sharp eye on him. She was happy when she saw him come straight from Lady De Courcy towards herself. Thorne, of course, was at her side, and to him Helver said, "Good evening, Doctor. Nice to see you again. May I borrow Eddie for the next dance?"

"Your Grace," Thorne replied, smiling. Being miffed with the Duke of Saymore, giver of the Tisbury living, formed no part of Thorne's plans. He was pleasantly surprised to hear him call Edgitha by so familiar a name. The Dame spoke of the relationship between the two, but this was the first sign he had seen of it. "We are honoured," he said.

"Eddie?" Helver said, offering his arm and biting back a setdown to the Doctor, who spoke of "we" as though he and Eddie were already a conjugal unit.

"You haven't been to the meadow all week, Eddie," he said as they walked away from the Doctor. "You said you usually go there afternoons."

"I couldn't get away. I don't think I'll be going there any more."

Helver heard this with a spasm of anger. "The Doctor has kept you well entertained taking you for drives, I collect. I am hearing strange rumours about you, young lady."

"There's a change. It is usually *I* who am hearing them about you."

"Is it true you're going to marry that old stick of a Thorne?"

"A thorn stick is for walking, not marrying," she quipped, but there was no smile for her efforts. "It is true he has asked me to marry him."

"But you have refused?"

"Not refused exactly. I haven't accepted either."

"You can't be serious! He's got grey hair at the temples, Eddie. A silly old man who runs around pouring his religious twaddle into matrons' ears. And the shuffling way he creeps about, like a reptile or a snake. What do you see in him?"

"Oh, but it is not *religious* twaddle he whispers in *my* ears," she teased.

"No, it is the best way to catch a frog or a mouse and swallow it whole, and when to shed your skin. All the best snake lore."

"Why do you call him a snake?" she asked, pleased at Helver's anger and trying to gauge the degree of jealousy in it.

"Because he reminds me of Satan in disguise. And not much of a disguise, either. Don't be an Eve and give in to him."

"I'll bear it in mind if he goes offering me any apples."

"Well, if he goes offering you the vicarage in Tisbury, you might remember *that* particular apple belongs to me, and don't think I mean to give him a job, for I don't."

This was joyful news to Edith, but she wished to make sure Helver was jealous and pretended to be vexed with him. "You won't find anyone better qualified. Everyone says he should get the post, and it will look very odd if you bring in an outsider with our own Doctor Thorne going begging."

"Our own Doctor Thorne may go to hell and damnation where he belongs. "*We* are honoured!" He thinks he *owns* you already." Edith smiled a smile that infuriated him, and he said, "Travers has found some old book about Tudor times for your mother. She'll send it over."

"Why don't you bring it?" Edith asked, remembering her mother's half-stated inference that respectable house calls were not entirely unacceptable and forgetting completely that Thorne was dying to get Helver to the Court.

"What, and have to sit and listen to old Thorne prose my ear off about gospels and sermons and theology? When does he leave?"

"Sunday."

"Would the Dame let me in, do you think?"

"She will not object."

"I could bring Lady Anne along for an excuse."

"You don't need an excuse to call on us, Helver."

"Since when?" he asked with a rueful smile. "You let the cat out of the bag the other day. You said she wouldn't mind if I brought Lady Anne. She doesn't like me, and who shall blame her."

Helver looked offended; Edith was angry with her mama but with Helver, too, for giving so much cause for minding. Between baronesses and bailiffs' wives he seemed always to give rise to gossip. "How is your affair with Milady going?"

"Poorly. Like the Congress of Vienna, *il ne marche pas, mais il danse.*"

"What?"

"Never mind. It would take us too deeply into French and politics."

"This is the first time she has ever come to one of our assemblies. I suppose you asked her to come?"

"Don't be absurd."

"I notice you stood up with her first, as soon as she got here."

"You will have noticed, as well, I hope, that she was with my aunt and uncle. It was a courtesy merely. Don't tell me you're jealous, Eddie?" he asked hopefully.

"Certainly not! She is excessively pretty. Much prettier than the Widow Malone was."

"But not nearly so pretty as Dame Durden's daughter," he smiled gallantly, and Edith flushed with pleasure. "Yes, you have even the Spanish ladies beat, I think. You look a little Spanish with your hair the way you wear it. If the Dame makes you get married, I'll be your *cavaliere servente,* shall I?"

"I only look Spanish, and I don't think Dorion would make a good don. Isn't that what they call the men there?" She was a little miffed that he followed up his compliments with a reference to her marrying someone else.

"Actually it's Italy that has the *cavaliere serventes,*" Helver said stiffly. He noticed that though he had not specified Thorne as a husband, he was the one who occurred to Edith. "But if you do marry Thorne, you'll need a lover for entertainment. That's what is done in the Latin countries. They make the young girls marry rich old men."

"Dorion isn't rich."

"All the more reason not to marry him, then. If you're old and ugly you ought at least to have some money or *something* to offer a girl."

"Dorion is very well bred."

"Eddie, don't try to gull me you care a hoot for all that Saxon stuff," he said impatiently. "That's your mother talking. Look at him now — there he is creeping around the floor with Blanche — Lady De Courcy — and a fine pair they make, too. Does he look like a purebred anything to you, except possibly a thoroughbred boa constrictor who wants to gobble her whole?" He was amazed to see that the Doctor was, in fact, smirking at Blanche in a way that lent some credence to her claim of having attached him.

Eddie looked and had to agree that his blood did very little to enhance his exterior, but she did not admit it aloud. Instead, she spoke about the useful and good life a vicar's wife would lead till Helver told her bluntly that it was the Dame Thorne ought to be offering for, for, if she thought *she* knew enough to be a helpmate to a Doctor of Divinity, she was crazy.

"Dorion doesn't think so!" she shot back, cut by this hurting truth.

Their dance was over, but Dorion stood with Lady De Courcy; and, as neither Eddie nor Helver was the least anxious to join them, they made the excuse of getting a glass of punch. He tried to bring forth some semblance of worth in himself by mentioning the brick homes he was building along the Avon, but this only called up the thought of Bessie Moog Sparks and Edith said, "I hear Bessie Sparks is to get a bigger one than all the others, and she doesn't even live on the river."

"Joe is my assistant bailiff, you know. He's an excellent chap."

"I know all about Joe Sparks. It's him you used to dash around with before you went away. He wasn't good for anything but drinking, riding like a demon and chasing girls with you."

"He's changed a lot. He's settled down amazingly since he's married to Bessie."

"Yes, and she is still very pretty, too!"

"That has nothing to do with it!"

"Hasn't it, Helver?"

"Certainly not! What are you hinting at, Eddie? What's happened to you lately? Has that holy creeper of a Thorne been filling your head with this sort of nonsense?"

"I don't need Dorion to tell me it's wrong to make Joe Sparks your bailiff and build him a big house only because you like Bessie."

Angered beyond civility, he said, "What can you expect of Bluebeard Trebourne?" and marched her promptly back to her doctor, to dance again himself with Lady De Courcy to spite her. If Bessie Sparks had been there, he would have danced with her, but, in her interesting condition, she was not well enough to attend the assembly.

Lady De Courcy achieved a victory over the village. Not only did the Duke of Saymore pay her more attention than was proper, but Sir Egbert, who had never been seen to dance since marrying Sara, stood up with her for a country dance also. She had one dance with Doctor Thorne and with Mr Hartman she had two. Sara didn't speak to Egbert for a week, and took out her ill humour in shouting at Helver. But though Lady De Courcy won an apparent victory, in her heart she knew she had lost the Duke of Saymore. Her most leading comments brought forth no rallying reply, no hint of visits to the little shelter she had found for herself to grow old in. When she told him at last that she was leaving in two days for London, he said, "Tisbury will miss you," and didn't ask for her address or whether she was coming back. She and Abbott walked the short distance home.

Edith had confirmed with her own eyes that Helver was in love with Milady — lust, as her mother called it — for he scarcely left her side for the whole last half of the dance. She thought she was a fool not to accept Doctor Thorne on the spot. She nearly did when he broached the matter again before leaving, but Helver had promised to come on Sunday, so she staved off Thorne with a mention that there was no hurry since he didn't have a living yet.

When Lady De Courcy's travelling carriage with the noble coat of arms on the door was hauled out from the stables at the inn and washed down for the trip, the village assumed she wasn't as crafty as they had thought to be running when she had such a grip on Helver. And she had got Lady Sara and Egbert to recognize her also. They regretted that the red-doored house on the corner would now be sunk to being only bricks and mortar like the others. Bessie Sparks's reputation took a jump — she was considered to be the cause of Milady's flight, and it was a great inconvenience that her house was so far removed from the village that they heard only secondhand if Helver's bay mount was seen tethered to the beech tree. With so little to amuse them they turned their interest on the vacant vicarage and determined to get themselves a vicar, for a cleric was always a ripe subject for scandal. If both he and his wife behaved themselves like common people, they could always be accused of lacking dignity; and, if Dorion and Edith took to putting on airs as people secretly hoped, there was plenty they could say about that, too. But first they had to get the vicarage occupied.

CHAPTER
TEN

In theory, the living of Tisbury and two others were the Duke of Saymore's to give as he saw fit. The last person in the world he wanted to give the vacancy to was Dorion Thorne, but he was being made aware by subtle pressures that the villagers expected and wanted Thorne to be their vicar. He could not walk down the main street without half a dozen of the good ladies asking him when they could expect to see Doctor Thorne in the pulpit. At home his mama, a Thorne supporter though she had never met the man, was as impatient as anyone else to be able to attend the service every Sunday instead of only every second Sunday, as they were doing at present. Mr Evans, the aging rector of St Michael's, made the fifteen-mile journey twice a month that the good people of Tisbury might hear the word of God and occasionally be christened, married or buried as the need arose. Thorne was standing by idle, perfectly prepared to fill the post, and unless he went outside the county, Helver knew of no one else to fill it. It had already been vacant too long. He had pretty well decided to offer it to Doctor Thorne when he told Eddie he wouldn't and, his angry statement to the contrary, he supposed he would do so.

He had still no desire to run into Thorne at the Court, however, and decided to wait till Sunday afternoon to make sure he was gone before hacking over with Travers's book for the Dame. On Sunday morning it was revealed to him that his mama had invited a few young ladies from the neighbourhood to amuse Lady Anne, and he was to be there to play host. It was an *al fresco* party his mother had had prepared, with considerable help from Travers and Sara. As is so often the case, the weather did nothing to add to the party's pleasure. It was not actually raining, but the skies were grey and the breeze chillier than was comfortable, so the party was transferred indoors. What was to have been an elegant picnic under the spreading elms turned into a scrambling sit-down luncheon. The guest of honour was smilingly silent but was not a great addition to the festivities, and the young ladies, having come prepared to be seduced by the greatest rake in England, were disappointed to find the host no more than tolerably friendly. The party was not a success, and by five o'clock the disappointed guests were happy enough to get into their carriages and go home.

Helver, who realized he should have had a very good time surrounded by a dozen pretty girls, was not only bored but fidgety. It was impossible to take Travers's book to the Dame, and he had told Edith he would. When the last carriage had left, he took his hack out for a fast ride before dinner.

Thorne had departed right after breakfast. When it got to be three o'clock, then four o'clock, and still Helver had not come, Edith realized he was not coming and told her mama she would take her mount out for a short ride before the storm broke.

"Mind you stay away from the east meadow," her mother cautioned.

"Don't worry, I will," was Edith's answer. Her pique this time was not directed against her mama. She was angry that Helver hadn't come. She cantered down to the public road towards Tisbury. In the distance she saw the shells of the brick cottages going up, and set her course in that direction. Sunday with the builders not present was a perfect chance to see them. She dismounted and began looking at the one closest to her. She was not the only visitor, and it was a matter of course that the families, still living in their thatched cottages only a stone's throw away, closer to the river, should be there in force inspecting progress. She fell into conversation with the family who was to occupy the particular dwelling she was looking at.

"How very nice this is," she said to Mrs Peters, who was smiling rapturously through a hole left in the brick for a window.

"It'll get the damp out of the cellars and the rats out of the roof," she was told with a satisfied smile. The woman went on to brag a little about her new home. "Here's to be our front room," she said, pointing to one corner of the undivided floor space presently laid with undressed lumber. "With a fireplace in the corner. And a second floor with *three* bedrooms, all with their own windows and a grate in my and the mister's room. Not that I'll think to light it every day, but the wind is chilly off the river in the wintertime. The Dook says it isn't fitting we should have the wee ones in our bedroom with us — he's a caution, for sure, that lad. He said to the mister — but I shouldn't be repeating it to a lady, I'm sure. Still, he's right."

It was left for Edith to imagine what indiscretion Helver had spouted about the ineligibility of children in the parents' bedroom; but, like the mother, Edith felt he was right about it. Trust him to think of that.

A dreamy look suffused the countrywoman's face. Life could offer her no more than such a house as this and plenty of children to fill the rooms on the second storey.

"It sounds very cosy," Edith congratulated her.

"It does surely," the woman answered, thinking "cosy" an inadequate word to describe her future luxury. "They may say what they will of Helver Trebourne — His Lordship, I ought to be calling him now — but he's a right one. He ain't full of starch and manners like the late Dook, but he's going to be all right. The old one didn't take such care of us. He may caper up a bit — well, he's young yet — but I didn't see the great old gaffer building us such homes as this. And now the young Dook is talking up a new school for the wee ones."

There was an ominous rumble of thunder, and Edith realized it was time to go home. A few drops of water began falling, and she looked about for a refuge. The old pavilion used for picnics was close by, overlooking the river, and she dashed towards it. She was no sooner under its roof than the shower came on hard, and before many more minutes she saw a horseman turn off the road and ride towards the building, seeking shelter like herself. His head was hunched into his collar, and it was by the mount rather than the man that she knew it to be Helver.

"What a day!" he said, removing his hat and shaking himself off as he ran up the steps under the roof. "You, too, were caught unawares, I see."

"Yes, but I don't think the shower will last long. It can't rain so hard for very long." The rain was lashing in at the open sides of the pavilion by this time.

There was some constraint between them after the near quarrel at the assembly, but, as Helver made no reference to it, Edith was determined to ignore it as well.

"Have you been out riding all alone, Eddie?" he asked as he looked around and saw it to be the case. "The Dame is getting lenient in her old age. You didn't used to be allowed on the public roads without a footman or groom."

"I just came out for a short ride and got caught in the rain."

"Has Thorne left?"

"Yes, quite early."

"I meant to call, but Mama had a party for Lady Anne, and it's just got over."

"I see," she replied, yet it occurred to her that, as he had time for a ride, there was nothing to prevent his having ridden towards Durden Court. "What sort of a party was it, to be over so soon?"

"A very boring party. A luncheon picnic that ended up in the house. It's too bad your mama won't let you

116

go to such affairs. I knew there was no point asking you."

"No, I couldn't have gone. A pity the weather ruined it. I've been down to see your new houses, Helver. They're very nice."

"Do you like them?" he asked eagerly. "I meant to stop by on my way home, but shan't have time now, very likely."

"They look lovely. It must be very expensive."

"It's costing an arm, but I can afford it. All this money that I'm looking after — well, it isn't really mine. I mean, if you have so much of everything, you have responsibilities to go along with it. Look at what happened in France because of the way the aristocracy treated the poor. Served them right to get their heads lobbed off. I was horrified to see how dark and damp the thatched cottages were, and half a dozen children crowded into one bedroom. What astonishes me is how they — the parents, I mean — didn't raise a fuss about it sooner. They're almost like children themselves, and someone must look after them. Oh, lord, don't I sound patronizing! I don't think I'm making myself very clear, am I?"

"I know what you mean."

"What I'm trying to say is they depend on me, and I have to look after them as though they were my family. We haven't a decent medical man in the whole community, only that snake-charmer of a Bieler. He's still recommending hanging garlic around your neck, for God's sake! I swear I saw little Jinny Pughe with a garlic around her neck, and she told me her mama told

117

her to wear it so she wouldn't catch a cold. And she running around the wet ground in her bare feet. I made all the parents take their children to the village and I paid for pattens for them, but getting them to wear them is something else."

"You were always interested in shoes. Do you remember when they made Peg Watkins go to Buxtons to tend the cows, you gave her a pair of shoes?"

"Yes, I thought of Peg at the time. I wonder what happened to her."

"She wears shoes now. I saw her in Tisbury — she's married, you know."

"That's good. I hope he's a decent fellow."

"Oh, yes — he has a little farm of his own. Mrs Peters tells me you might do something about a new school."

"Yes, but first I must get a doctor — a *real* one — and heaven only knows where I'll find one. I'm advertising in the papers. The school will be next. The children aren't getting any kind of education, between leaving school in the good weather to pick stones for the roads and in the bad weather not being able to stand the draughty little building they call a school. There isn't a footman or serving girl at the Hall that knows how to read. I asked Billie to fetch me *The Observer* the other day, and he brought me *The Farmer's Almanac*. I hadn't realized till then the appalling ignorance. And, of course, there is the matter of a vicar for the local church," he added, with a sudden quizzing smile.

"You're quite overburdened with it all," Edith answered, only half joking.

"It's a lot more work and responsibility than I ever counted on, for I never did a hand's turn in my life till after my father died. And I haven't been next or nigh my other two places yet. I have to make time to get over to Ratton Hall next week, and there are two days gone. Luckily I can count on Forringer and Sparks to see to things here. You will notice I don't speak of sending Joe over to Ratton Hall so that I may make free with his wife, and don't say it didn't occur to you because I saw that look in your eyes."

"I notice it *occurred* to you, too."

"Am I to be held accountable for every thought that flits into my head? In that case I might as well hand Satan my soul and be done with trying to make anything of myself."

Edith was happy, greatly relieved to see Helver settling down, trying to make something of himself, as he had said, perhaps without realizing he said it. In her heart she had always thought he would one day stop chasing girls. She looked at him with approval and just a little sorrow that he had to grow up so fast. It was so odd to hear him discuss serious problems. His greatest worry had been whether his nag had sprained a tendon, or his new jacket hadn't one sleeve longer than the other, or whether his books would arrive from London. "You hardly have a minute for your flirts," she said lightly, but she knew it wasn't really a matter for lightness.

"Oh, I ain't *that* busy!" he assured her, very much in his old way. "Still, I sometimes wish I was plain Mr Smith and could move into one of those little homes I'm building and let someone else do the worrying. They're going to be snug little homes, Eddie, with a front room looking out on the Avon. Wouldn't it be nice to live there with no worries but getting the hay in and seeing the cows didn't get into the garden? We'd put the children to bed early and sit in front of our fire; you could bring me a glass of ale and my pipe, and sit at my feet while I complained of my sore back."

"Don't we have two chairs, Helver?"

"Even a settle if you like, but, mind, you'd have to upholster it yourself."

"And couldn't we have just one servant to bring us both a glass of ale?"

He looked at her with his brows raised and a teasing smile. "I'm not sure I like my wife to be drinking ale. It will make her fat and so will having a maid to do her chores for her. Mrs Smith is getting ideas above her station. Next she'll be wanting a gig and pony to show off to the neighbours."

"Oh, but I mean to raise my own chickens and save the egg money to buy the pony. And maybe if the Duke of Saymore takes a fancy to you — or me," she added with a saucy smile, "he'll make you his assistant bailiff, and we can take a trip to Bath."

Helver raised a hand in protest. "Reality begins to intrude. You're ruining my charming idyll, hussy. I was picturing just the two of us, with the world locked out."

"No man is an island. Who was it that said that?"

"I don't know, but he was right."

The wind blew around the struts of the building, and they moved farther into the centre of the pavilion. "It's cold," Edith said, with a little shiver.

"If you weren't Dame Durden's daughter, I'd offer to warm you," Helver said and laughed as she walked farther away from him.

"Well, I *am* Dame Durden's daughter."

"You don't have to remind me. Did you give old Thorne his answer before he left?"

"No."

"He's patient. When will you tell him?"

"When I decide."

"It's considered quite a settled thing in the village. If you don't mean to have him, you ought to say so."

"Who said I don't mean to have him?"

"Lord, what a husband *he'd* make!"

"Much you know about it! He'd make a very good husband."

"If I give him a job."

Edith pouted and looked away towards the river. Helver walked off to the other side and began whistling, as though forgetful of her presence. After a few moments the shower stopped, and a few gigs were seen to pass by on the road. "It's stopped raining," Helver pointed out.

"I'd best go. Mama will be worried."

"Especially if she knew you were with Bluebeard Trebourne," he added sardonically.

"Yes, people would be taking me for your new flirt." Helver gave her a long, serious look that made her uncomfortable; and, just to have something to say, she asked if he planned to go to London that spring.

"Not this Season. Haven't I just been telling you how busy I am and have to go to Ratton Hall next week? I don't think you take my reformation very seriously."

"You said you still find time for your flirts."

"Well, I lied. I'm so tired at night I'm not good for anything. I expect my hair will start silvering any day. Next thing I know my spine will stiffen, and people will start calling me 'Dook'."

"They've already started. Mrs Peters called you that today."

"Did she though?" he asked, rather pleased with this recognition of his eminence.

She nodded. "She said you'd make a good one, too."

"I mean to," he answered simply, looking very young and forlorn with his wet hair falling across his forehead, his collar turned up around his neck. Looking at him across the pavilion, Edith felt she wanted to cry. Instead, she smiled a sad, wistful smile.

Helver regarded her levelly, then walked a half dozen steps towards her. "Don't let the Dame push you into marrying him, Eddie. He's not good enough for you."

She waited to hear if he had any other suggestion to make, but, as he only went on looking, she said, "I'd best go."

She did not see fit to tell her mama that Helver had been with her in the pavilion, but before many hours the Dame discovered the fact for herself. The eyes of those passing in the gigs had been well occupied to discover the young people talking together. It was first assumed that the young lady was Bessie Sparks, but the mare tied to the railing had let out the secret, and before nightfall it was said in the village that Helver had another girl trailing after him. That nice little Edith Durden. Who'd have thought it of her, and she practically the Doctor's wife?

Dame Durden was a strict parent, but she was not an unreasonable one. She felt she was well justified in protecting her only child from the lures of the local rake, and every daughter's mother would have agreed with her. The meetings in the meadow had frightened her since they were not accompanied by the customary courting a serious attachment would have been. When she thought Edith to have been sneaking out behind her back despite her warnings, the Dame was seriously alarmed and laid down the law.

When she returned from Tisbury the next day she said, "I've heard from no less than three women in the village today of your meeting Helver at the pavilion yesterday, Edith."

"It was an accident. We were only there a minute, to get out of the rain."

"These accidental meetings occur too often to please me, and I must doubt their innocence when you hide them from me. Why did you not tell me?"

"I knew you'd be upset over nothing, Mama."

"Well, I am upset, and I don't call it nothing that my own daughter has turned deceitful on me. This time I mean to take action. You'll accept Doctor Thorne before you become the scandal of the village. To hear you spoken of in the same breath as that De Courcy woman and Bessie Sparks! 'I thought it must be Bessie Sparks,' Mrs Connery told me with her sly eye laughing at me. 'Imagine my surprise to see it was Miss Durden.' If he meant to do the right thing, he'd come to the door like a gentleman and not be sneaking off to meet you in corners."

"We weren't sneaking off!"

"No, and you'll not be sneaking off. I hope I know my duty. Did he ever mention a word of marrying you? No," she answered her own question, and her daughter could not deny it.

"I'm writing Dorion this day to say you accept, Edith. For your own good."

"He has no position."

"He'll soon get one. I suppose Helver has been holding back on purpose to keep Dorion from being in a position to marry. Well, Tisbury isn't the only living in England. A man of Doctor Thorne's attainments might do better than a little church with a salary of three hundred pounds."

"It's not that. Helver just doesn't like Dorion."

"No, Joe Sparks is who *he* likes and never mind why."

"It's not true. He has nothing to do with Bessie."

"Did he tell you so?"

"Yes."

"I suppose he told you he hadn't been near the De Courcy woman either, and the whole village clocking him in and out. He's not good for you, Edith. Forget him. I'm writing Dorion, and in half a year's time you'll be thanking me when Helver is out chasing some other chit."

"I think he's changing, Mama."

The Dame looked at her sharply. "What do you mean? Does he ever speak to you of marriage? Do you think that's what he has in his mind?"

Edith thought he had been going to speak about it when he asked her not to marry Dorion, but he hadn't. No, what he really meant was that he still found time for his flirts. Maybe not Bessie Sparks but certainly Lady De Courcy, and certainly another after her if she left. Edith had been waiting too long for him to grow up. Well, he had shouldered his ducal responsibilities just as he ought, but he did not mention marrying herself or anyone else. "No, I imagine that is not what he has in mind," she confessed and felt ashamed of her foolishness, and angry at Helver for making her ashamed.

"I'll write Dorion, then," the Dame said and looked to see if Edith objected.

She sat a moment, then said, "All right, Mama. Write him that I accept." Her voice was firm, not wavering in the least; but it was a strange, hard voice in which to be accepting a proposal of marriage. It was with a heavy heart that the Dame wrote the letter, but she wrote it.

Helver rode home from the pavilion to be railed at for the roof (still not fixed) and the rain pouring in. After dinner he locked himself in his office to get away from the family. He looked out on nearly total darkness, for the Hall sat in a vast park of private acres. Only a new moon showed the dark outline of trees against the paler sky. The scraggly pines stood above all the others, with here and there an elm recognized by its spreading branches or a willow by its leafy arms dragging down to the ground. These few weeks of Helver's life had been strange for him. He had first disliked to be so shackled with work, especially as he was so ill-prepared for it. But with Forringer's help he was beginning to take the reins in his own hands, to take an interest in the doings of his "people," as he was beginning to consider them. His obligations, though onerous, were satisfying; and it was with a feeling of accomplishment that he returned to the Hall at night. He would almost liked to have stayed there, for it was tiring to arise at seven o'clock and be in the saddle or office till six o'clock, but the atmosphere at home was not congenial. There were the relatives nagging, and now Anne looking at him as though he ought to be playing with her. So he went out but with decreasing enjoyment of his old haunts. Even the dashing Milady had not amused him as formerly she would have. And it was not her lack of cooperation alone that was held to blame. That might have been overcome, he thought, had he considered it worth the while.

No, what he would really like to do nights was sit in front of a grate with just one pretty woman to talk to, to pet and cosset him and perhaps compliment him a little. The poorest farmer had that. Such a woman, of course, must be a wife; and though he had abhorred the idea of getting married, he came to see that, at a certain time in a man's life, it was not only a possible thing to consider, but a positive desire. More and more frequently in his mind the woman sitting at his feet was Eddie Durden. He could not have said exactly when this old playmate had turned into a wanted wife, but somehow it had happened. When she had cocked her head at him and said, "Well, I am a girl, Helver," perhaps that was the beginning of it. At least from then on he had been very much aware that she was a female, and she hadn't always seemed particularly like one. That she was a *femme fatale* was only a joke, but that she had a very eager suitor in Doctor Thorne was no joke. Quite the contrary. And she always spoke highly of him, so she must have at least some regard for the man.

Helver had been within a breath of asking her to marry him that afternoon in the pavilion, and he thought she might accept. But the Dame must be softened up first. With a girl like Eddie, things had to be done properly. He would go to the door with his hat in hand and tell the Dame the news. She might very likely throw him out, but at least he'd try to do the thing properly, and, if he had to, he'd elope with her. But first he'd try the right way. She had been in no hurry to accept Thorne, so she couldn't be in love with him. He'd take the book over tomorrow and formally ask the Dame for permission to court Edith. And he'd return next day and every day till the Dame grew so tired of looking at his mongrel face that she would let him marry Eddie to be rid of him.

CHAPTER
ELEVEN

Mrs Hartford, the mother of Miss George, was passing by Durden Court that same day and stopped in for the sole purpose of seeing what she could discover about Edith and Helver Trebourne. Her interpretation of their meeting was that they had gone jauntering down the public road together, disappearing into an empty house. With such a story as this going the rounds, Dame Durden was happy to be able to say that Edith had just accepted an offer of marriage from Doctor Thorne, and the one meeting with the Duke of Saymore had been an accidental one at the public pavilion to escape the rain. She wondered if what Edith had told her was true. The fact was she no longer trusted her daughter one hundred percent, as she used to, especially where Helver was concerned. She couldn't say that Edith had actually lied to her, but she had concealed the truth, which was nearly as bad. Mrs Hartford's news pleased the villagers, and it was of Edith's marriage rather than her disgrace that they spoke the rest of the day.

Even a Duke of Saymore bent on getting engaged had his usual duties to perform; and it was not till late afternoon, after his round with Forringer, that he went to the Court. The Dame sat with her daughter in the parlour and was determined she would not move an inch throughout the visit. The book was given to her and dutiful thanks offered. A glance at the cover told her it was useless. How could anyone be so ignorant as to think Richard the Lion-hearted, a Plantagenet, was a Tudor? The business and pretext for the visit over, Helver sought to put the meeting on a friendlier footing before broaching his real reason for calling.

"Here it is May first and no May Day revels, Dame Durden," he ventured, smiling.

"I hope next year we may reinstitute them," she said and forged on to let him know of the wedding. "Once Edith and Doctor Thorne are married we will have someone other than myself to take an interest in those historical events. Dorion is greatly interested in my project of restoring the past."

Having heard as late as yesterday that the wedding was not definite, Helver asked, "Do you think they will be married by next year, then?"

"Long before that," the Dame said firmly. "Edith has accepted his offer, and we mean to do it this spring."

She hoped to surprise Helver but had not expected to shock him so that he started from his chair. "But you haven't accepted!" he said to Edith in a very loud voice.

Edith just sat looking mute and miserable, and it was for the Dame herself to enlighten him. "Yes, his offer was accepted today. We have invited him back to the Court and mean to settle the time and all details immediately."

"You said you hadn't made up your mind!" Helver continued, listening to the Dame but addressing himself to Edith.

"She has made up her mind now," Dame Durden said.

"Have you, Edith?" he asked bluntly, his voice incredulous. Really, he was an astonishingly rude young man.

Edith looked at him, and at her mother, and said, "Yes, I have accepted Dorion's offer today."

"Why?" he asked, clearly astonished.

"What a question!" the Dame declared. "For all the usual reasons, Helver. Because he is a very respectable gentleman, from a good family, well educated and with good prospects. And because she admires and respects him."

"But she doesn't love him!" he said, turning to the Dame.

"Love comes later. You young people do too much prating about love and don't even know what it is."

"I know what it is," Edith said in a flat little voice.

"Oh, yes, one of your great experience is bound to know all about it," her mother said in an ironic tone. "It has nothing to do with that poetry you read, Edith. It isn't liking a handsome face, or admiring a man's shoulders. Faces age and shoulders sag, but character goes on being straight or crooked and that is what a woman loves if she has any sense; and if she hasn't, then she has no right to be getting married." She named no names, but both Helver and Edith knew to what handsome face she referred, and what crooked character.

All Helver's plans were knocked out of his head by the announcement just made, and he found himself saying, "Can I see Eddie alone, Dame Durden?"

"That is not necessary, Helver," was his answer.

He arose and marched angrily to the door. Both women thought he was about to leave without even saying goodbye, but he stopped just at the doorway and turned back to them, his eyes flashing and his face hard with anger. "Has he got a living yet?" he asked.

"No, not yet," the Dame answered.

"Good."

"The Tisbury living . . ." Mrs Durden began, eager to get Dorion settled.

"It's taken," he said abruptly.

"Taken! Who have you given it to?"

"Hanley Barton."

"That scoundrel!" Mrs Durden scoffed. "You mustn't think of it. He's nothing but a horse trader, no more interested in the church than is a squirrel."

"You forget, Dame Durden, he is my cousin and has been in holy orders for two years." Helver had grabbed the name out of the air, or nearly so. Hanley had occurred to him only to be rejected as unsuitable. He was simply determined not to set Dorion up to marry Eddie.

"You bring that fellow into the church and you won't have a soul in the congregation. It's time you faced up to your duties as a Christian and as the lord of this village, Helver Trebourne. You're old enough to cut out your pranks and your sprees."

The Dame was accustomed to speaking to young Helver in this fashion and not yet accustomed to remembering he was now the Duke of Saymore. She was reminded forcibly of the fact at this moment, for he stared at her, not in fear and submission as the young boy used to but with an arrogant sneer on his mature face. "Old enough to know my duty, ma'am, and do it without your reminding. Old enough to give you a piece of advice as well. The living of Tisbury is in my giving, and it is no part of my duty to provide your son-in-law a job. If you wish favours of me, you will do well in future to petition through the usual channels."

"We're not begging favours!" she shot back angrily.

"And you're certainly not doing me any," he said, then went out the door without a backward glance.

"So that's what he's up to," the Dame said to her daughter. "Bringing Hanley Barton to Tisbury to racket around the countryside with him, ruining horses and girls."

"You shouldn't have spoken so to him, Mama. He's no longer a little boy."

The Dame opened her mouth to give argument but closed it without speaking. She had made a tactical error to mention Dorion when Helver was so angry. She had to wonder at his anger, his very apparent shock at hearing Edith was to marry Dorion. From his expression it almost seemed he loved her. But if he wanted to marry her, why had he contrived to meet her secretly in meadows and pavilions? No, it must be that he was angry to have his flirt snatched from him; and, if that was the game he was playing, Edith must marry Dorion without a moment's delay. And how were they to marry without a position for Dorion? He was too proud to come and live with them — *off* them, for that is what it would amount to. If he didn't get the Tisbury living, he couldn't possibly stay in the vicinity. She had not thought to see Edith, her only child, move far away from her. For herself to leave the Court was equally impossible. She lived not only in Durden Court but for it. She was faced with a bad kettle of fish, and the only solution, much as she loathed it, was to conciliate Helver in some manner.

For two days the Dame worried over her *faux* pas in annoying Helver; Edith waited in dreadful suspense for Dorion to visit them again; and Helver fretted that he had been unforgivably rude to Eddie's mother. He had needlessly turned her against him even more than usual. He went over every word of the interview a dozen times, with particular emphasis on Edith's gestures, for she had said very little. He couldn't believe she wanted to marry Dorion. This was a scheme of the Dame's, and he must thwart it. But with this foolish quarrel he had made it impossible to even see Eddie. He wrote a note to Dorion offering the post of Vicar of Tisbury. He had never liked Thorne and was rapidly coming to hate him with a white-hot intensity, but he would not allow him to be the cause of a rupture between himself and the Durdens. It was expected by the whole village that he appoint Dorion to the

Vicarage; and, as the Dame had said, it was time he assumed his duties.

Foreseeing a prolonged stay at the Court, Dorion had taken a few days to assemble his gear, and the note from Helver arrived before he left. One of the first to hear of Thorne's arrival at Tisbury was Helver, for he sent a note over to the Hall the minute he arrived asking permission to call and express his thanks in person for the great honour, etcetera. It was not without some apprehension that the Duke decided to use Thorne's appointment as an excuse to call again at the Court. They could hardly refuse entrance when he came as a benefactor, and he was eager for any pretext to see Eddie. Frequent rides through the meadow had shown him she was not inclined, or perhaps not allowed, to go there.

It was four o'clock in the afternoon when Helver tethered his bay to the fence post and walked up the cobblestone walk to the studded oak door of the Court. He found Doctor Thorne, Edith and the Dame having tea in the parlour. There was a tension between the group, a wondering on both sides as to how much offence had been given, and, on Helver's, how much forgiveness had been bought with the position of Vicar for Thorne. The smiles that greeted him relieved him of the fear of not being welcome. The Dame and the Doctor were both in spirits, but he noticed at a glance that Eddie wasn't smiling. He was made welcome by Dame Durden, but Thorne did not consider her welcome sufficient and undertook to add his own.

"You had my note, Your Grace," he went on.

"Yes, and decided to drop by to save you the trip, as I was in the vicinity. I am happy you have accepted the post offered."

"It is I who am happy — delighted, I might say, at your generosity, and coming so opportunely, too," he added, smiling at Edith.

"I'm afraid it's not the sort of a post that a man with your qualifications merits. Tisbury is a small congregation; the vicarage only a four-bedroom cottage and the salary, as I mentioned, three hundred a year."

"The cottage is charming. Very charming, and Edith will smarten it up. I have often been to visit the late Vicar there and thought the house had definite possibilities."

"It is a pleasant little place — large enough for newlyweds. The garden is quite large, which will perhaps help to cover the expense of food."

"As a clergyman, Your Grace, material advantages are not my first consideration. The salary is high for such a small congregation. Very generous, indeed. I have some familiarity with the people hereabouts, for my own home is only twelve miles away, and I have often preached a sermon here in the past. Edith, of course, is known to them all and will be a helpmeet to me."

Helver was forced to swallow his bile at these constant references to Edith as the vicar's wife. While they talked, Edith poured the Duke a cup of tea and added milk and two teaspoons of sugar, knowing his preference from the past. He observed her out of the corner of his eye and looked to see if Thorne had noticed. It was a small detail but the sort of thing that would have infuriated him if his bride had done it for another man.

"You have a good memory, Eddie," he said, tasting it. "You remembered exactly how I take my tea."

"Oh, yes, I remember," she said, and Thorne smiled with satisfaction.

"A good memory is a great advantage in a vicar's wife," was his comment. "I hope you will often take tea with us at the cottage, Your Grace."

"I hope I am often invited," he answered calmly.

"You must feel free to come whenever you wish," Thorne followed it up immediately. "As Vicar of your village, I consider myself as something of a moral mentor to yourself. You do not have a domestic chaplain, I believe?"

"No, I have not felt the need of one."

"I shall undertake to hold myself at your disposal in any matters you wish to discuss with me."

"I'll bear it in mind," Helver said, becoming angrier by the moment at the man's condescension.

There was some discussion as to when Thorne would assume his duties. The coming Sunday was chosen, as Thorne was eager and the villagers most anxious, to get services regularized.

It was clear there would be no private conversation with Edith, and Helver soon arose to take his leave. He was scarcely out the door when Thorne arose and rubbed his hands together. "I like him excessively," he said to the Dame and her daughter. "It was very civil in him to call. Quite a mark of respect."

136

"He can be civil when he wishes," Dame Durden replied. "I wonder what made him change his mind about giving the post to Hanley Barton."

"I shouldn't be surprised if we have Edith to thank for that," Thorne said, with an appreciative smile at his bride. "It is quite clear he likes you. That was clever, remembering how he takes his tea. That is the very sort of thing that makes him aware of his own importance, you know. These noble fellows like to be considered a little above the general run of mankind. It does no harm to pander to their vanities in such matters."

"He's always been close to Edith," Dame Durden agreed, for Edith was sitting silently, with a mutinous lift to her chin. The Dame decided Helver had given Dorion the post because of Edith, because of their past friendship. He had seemed very angry at the marriage, but his better nature had won out and he decided to help her. She was greatly relieved to have it all settled so satisfactorily.

In her corner, Edith looked at Dorion and wondered how she had ever thought she could marry him. Though he had come to the Court as a would-be bridegroom, there was nothing of the lover in his manner. It discommoded neither himself nor Edith that the Dame was usually with them, and, in fact, Edith was extremely sorry when her mama arose and left the room. Dorion continued discussing Helver in the same vein as before.

"Your being on such a footing with the Duke of Saymore is an excellent circumstance," he said.

"I doubt many gentlemen would say that to their brides, Dorion," she countered. "He has quite a reputation with the ladies, you must know."

"I know it well, and it is not only the low-born village girls he runs after, either. He had the infernal impudence to pester Lady De Courcy with his advances. We may count on his discretion to treat a vicar's wife with propriety, however. And even if his character is not what one could wish of a duke, that is nothing to us. As a friend, a patron, he will be very useful."

Edith's back was already up to hear that Helver should respect her for marrying Thorne, whom he hated; and, when the cold-blooded word "useful" was added she could not control her response. "Helver has always treated me with respect, and as to his being *useful*, I trust we have not imposed on his friendship. Mama would not have suggested his giving you the job if you were not so eminently suited for it."

"As to that, suitability would mean nothing to *him*. You may be sure getting a suitable candidate had no part in his decision. No, he did it to oblige *you*, and I find his mention of the salary being low interesting. You might drop him a hint we could do with another hundred."

"You told him the salary was *high* for a small parish. I can't ask him for more."

"Not *ask* in so many words. A little subtlety will be required. A hint that you will be purse-pinched, a small complaint dropped here and there as to the things you will have to do without; and see if he doesn't come up with an increase, without your even suggesting it."

"But we won't be purse-pinched. We'll have the house and the garden, the three hundred salary and my dowry."

"Oh, as to your dowry, Edith," he said with a tone of disparagement, "I think the Dame might have done better than ten thousand pounds. The only child . . ."

This from a man without a single penny of his own to his name! "You must drop *her* a hint *you* will be purse-pinched, Dorion. You stand quite as high in that quarter as I do with Saymore."

He had the hide of an elephant and, rather than taking offence, sat considering her suggestion a moment. "With another hundred *per annum* we might set up a carriage," was his reply.

"I hadn't thought you to be so interested in worldly goods," she said, highly vexed. His talk had always been of moral matters. This quest for wealth was new.

"A man likes to treat his wife as well as he can. For myself, I shouldn't care if I ever had a carriage, but you are accustomed to one."

This mollified her somewhat, but she was quick to point out that the carriage was a matter of indifference to her.

"Still, I think you should at least drop him a hint," he persisted. "There can be no harm in that. And another thing; Evans is getting on in years. When he is put to pasture, I think I could handle St Michael's as well as my own congregation."

"Dorion, the two parishes are fifteen miles apart. You know both churches have made do with a service every second Sunday since our Vicar died. One man can't handle two churches."

"A young man could. Evans is nudging seventy. I shouldn't mind running them both. St Michael's brings in two hundred and fifty a year."

"Well, *I* should mind having you work so hard. To be running back and forth, having one service too early at one church and the other too late. It is nonsense."

"Still, he might do it for *you*."

"What about the people? How could you tend to the spiritual needs of two congregations? And with livings short, someone else ought to be given a chance. This is carrying greediness too far."

He was immediately on his high ropes. "You have misunderstood me, Edith. With two salaries, we would be in a better position to perform charitable works."

"Yes, like setting ourselves up with a carriage!" she replied angrily.

"I don't see why ministers of the church should go on foot, while every merchant and journeyman in the county is setting himself up with a carriage or gig. It gives the people a poor idea of our dignity. How is a man to gain the respect of his people if he goes about in rags and on foot?"

"How are the people to think you are interested in spiritual matters if you set about aping the ways of rich merchants? I never thought you were so vain."

"It has nothing to do with vanity. You don't see a dean or a bishop going anywhere on foot. But my first thought now must always be of you. I don't want to see my wife walking along the dusty roads to visit the poor."

"I think I have made it quite clear I have no objection to walking," she said firmly and glared at him. There was a defiance in her manner entirely new to her. She hoped to bring the engagement to a termination: She acknowledged it honestly to herself, and Dorion was clever enough to suspect it.

Breaking with Edith when she had just proved such a prime favourite with the Duke of Saymore was the farthest thing from Thorne's mind, and he began to speak of other things. He discussed a theological conference he had lately attended and impressed her with his show of learning. For the remainder of the day he said not a word about St Michael's.

The next day he drove uninvited over to the Hall to thank His Grace in person once more for the honour bestowed and to assure him in all humility that he meant to do all within his powers to bring grace and peace on his parishioners.

Helver heard him out with impatience and wondered that Eddie should marry such a humbug. "I'm sorry the salary isn't higher," the Duke said as he walked the

Vicar to the door. Somehow the matter had arisen, ever so subtly, between them.

"The financial rewards are nothing to me," the Vicar assured him, "though I shall, of course, be sorry I can't set up a carriage for my wife."

"Eddie will have to get used to walking," Helver replied with a smile and a certain knowledge of what that sly dig meant.

"Yes, and doing without new gowns and bonnets," Dorion continued, looking closely to note the response to this tack.

"It might be best to put off the nuptials till you are better situated," Helver mentioned with a lessening of his smile.

"Oh, no! We are eager to get on with it. I hope you will do us the honour to attend our wedding, Your Grace."

"I don't mean to miss Eddie's wedding. When is it to be?"

"The last Saturday of June. We shall send you a card."

"Perhaps I'll give the bride away. She has no father to do it for her."

"That would be very kind of you," Thorne answered, greatly pleased with the notion.

"I'll talk it over with Eddie and the Dame and see what they think."

Thorne was deep in concentration as he drove back to the Court. That his bride was called Eddie by the Duke filled him with glee. He spoke of her almost as a sister, or better, girl friend, and, if that couldn't be put to advantage, he wasn't Dorion Q. Thorne. He felt Edith could wind the fellow round her thumb if only she weren't such a little fool.

In the vestibule, Travers was lying in wait for Helver and asked him at once what he thought of Doctor Thorne as a new vicar.

"He's a jackanapes, if you want the truth. I can't imagine what Eddie sees in him."

"What the Durdens see in him isn't visible to the naked eye. Blood — Saxon blood. Of course, it is all the Dame's doings. It must be."

"It is the Dame pushing the match, but she wouldn't make Eddie have him. Would she?" A little frown creased his brow.

Travers weighed her answer carefully. An affirmative would clinch Helver's marrying Edith. A heroine being forced into a loveless marriage would appeal strongly to him; but, as there was a definite possibility that Edith *wanted* to marry Thorne, she would not like to throw the girl into the path of being kidnapped and dragged to Gretna Green, which she well knew Helver was capable of doing. On the other hand, she suspected that Edith had always loved Helver and was becoming more and more convinced that the feeling was now reciprocated. "Why don't you ask her?" she compromised.

"I will," he said and walked away frowning harder than ever. He was absent-minded throughout dinner, so Travers didn't give up hope of yet seeing her favourite settled to her satisfaction.

Helver didn't go out that evening. He went early to his room and thought over the turn events were taking. He couldn't believe Edith loved Thorne, but he couldn't believe either that she would have become engaged to him unless she was determined to marry him. She was a prim little lady; and breaking an engagement, especially to a churchman like Thorne, was not the sort of activity indulged in by well-bred young ladies. He would tread softly, for a change. There was a month till the wedding. Anything could happen in a month.

CHAPTER
TWELVE

On Sunday Helver had the experience, which he did not consider a pleasure, of having his benevolence bruited from the pulpit by Doctor Thorne. The learned Doctor spoke long, for, in addition to a sermon he wrote to display his erudition and eloquence, he had to say several words regarding his benefactor. He had worked out a laboured analogy featuring himself as the shepherd of the flock, with the Duke the man hiring the shepherd. Butter was poured over everyone, from employer to shepherd to sheep. There never was a better flock, and never one in such good hands, either, both temporal and spiritual. It was when Dorion was in the pulpit that Edith would think she could marry him, but today she took no pleasure in his speech. To hear him publicly praise Helver, whom he abused in private, was extremely annoying. After the service and a good deal of hand shaking and complimenting — for the good people of Tisbury found no fault in the speech — the two guides, temporal and spiritual, were to repair to Durden Court for luncheon. This had been Doctor Thorne's idea. He meant to foster the friendship between the families to the utmost of his considerable abilities.

Being six years older than the fatherless Duke, he hoped to stand in as a sort of father for the boy in managing his various affairs, but was soon disabused of this idea. "I would be happy to give the Beadle a hand in the matter of the parish boys," he began, referring to the orphans. "As they assist at my services, I will come to know them well, and there is no need for the Parish Officer to be running to you every time he has a truant on his hands."

"No need to run to *you*, either, Doctor Thorne," Helver replied. "If the Parish Officer and the Beadle between them can't handle such a small matter, they are incompetent and must be replaced." Then turning to Dame Durden with a smile he said, "I haven't tasted roast bitterns and Lumbard fritters since I left home, Ma'am. I think yours must be the last house in Wiltshire that still serves them."

"The old ways are good enough for me," she answered, pleased with the compliment.

"Nowhere else in England could one sit down to such a meal as this," Thorne said, to outdo him in praise.

"How are the houses along the edge of the river coming, Helver?" Dame Durden enquired after a little.

"The brickwork is coming along nicely. Nothing much has been done inside yet. It's hard to get well-qualified workmen."

"That is a vastly expensive project you are taking on," Thorne mentioned. With so much money to throw around, another two hundred a year would never be missed, he was thinking. "I don't think it does to spoil

146

those good, simple people. If I might proffer a suggestion, Your Grace, could the men and women not do the interior work themselves, during the winter months when their farm labour is not great?"

"No, I don't want shoddy amateur work; it is a job for carpenters and stone-layers. The craftsmen can well use the work; it is only that, with so many homes being built at one time, they are busy."

"I should have contented myself with replacing one or two of the worst and let the others be for the present."

"My bailiff and I considered all alternatives. It was less costly to have done with it all at one time. Ordering the materials in large quantities was less expensive, and also saved time."

"As to a bailiff, I shouldn't put myself totally in his hands till I had a good notion of his character, Your Grace. They are only mortals, like the rest of us, and subject to human failings. There is no saying he isn't looking to make a profit on such a transaction himself. There must have been a great quantity of materials purchased, and workers contracted and so on. Very likely he has taken advantage of your inexperience in such matters and made himself a handsome profit under the table."

"It is not my custom to put myself totally in anyone's hands. We took the decision together, Forringer and I, and, as he has been with the family for forty years, serving us faithfully, it's not likely he's turned criminal at this late date."

Edith thought how ironic it was, and how revealing of his true feelings, that Dorion should speak as he did after just praising the common people in the pulpit an hour before.

"Still, you must step cautiously, Your Grace," Thorne went on. "You will forgive my taking such a liberty, but you are young, and, as I am your spiritual mentor . . ." Helver shot a discouraging glance towards the speaker at this piece of imprudence but held his tongue, and Thorne went on, "I feel it incumbent on me to point out the possible pitfalls."

"I interpret your duties quite otherwise, Doctor. You should more properly restrict yourself to spiritual matters."

"Yes, very true, Your Grace. Spiritual matters are the very gist of my calling. There is no argument there. I agree with you on that score, but, as an older man with some experience in these affairs, I would feel myself remiss not to point out to you that a large building undertaking is a chance for double dealing. I never knew one yet to come in under the budget."

"Your experience in construction cannot be much greater than my own, Doctor. Surely you didn't do your thesis on the construction business."

"Ha, ha, you make a fast joke, Your Grace." Helver felt that, if he was called "Your Grace" once more at that table, he would be required to arise and leave. "No, indeed, I did my thesis on incipient heterodoxy in the Church of England. An interesting subject. I will be happy to discuss it with you, at your convenience. But as an older man . . ."

"Now take care, Doctor. You will be giving your bride the idea she is marrying an old man."

"He didn't say *old*, he said older. Older than you is what he meant," Edith said, rather sharply. Her anger was vented at Helver, but it was really her fiancé she was peeved with. Why must he be so officious when it was clear Helver wanted no help from him? She had wanted Dorion to appear in a good light, but it was his worst foot that was going forward at every step. At least he didn't mention wanting a higher salary.

Helver left as early as was polite after lunch. He found the Doctor intolerable.

"He's not as biddable as I'd hoped," was Doctor Thorne's comment when he sat with his bride in the parlour.

"He is not biddable at all," Edith told him. "You have only to say 'black' to anything for Helver to say 'white' at once."

"You know him very well, Edith. You'll know just how to manage him. He didn't take to me much. It is you who must get the St Michael's living for us. Best mention it when I'm not around, or he'll think I put you up to it."

"I have no intention of conniving behind his back. He has given you Tisbury Church. That will have to do for the present."

"Oh, yes, it will do for the *present*. Don't push him too hard. He's too good a patron to lose. I heard at Salisbury when I was at the Conference that the Dean had been to see him. He might do something for me in that quarter, if we can keep him interested in us."

Edith kept all her disgust to herself except such bits as escaped through her flashing eyes and flouncing shoulders when she went to get her pelisse to go to Tisbury, to go through her future home.

"Here will be my study," Dorion said, standing in the middle of the front parlour.

"This was always the late Vicar's parlour," Edith told him. "The study is the little room at the back there, facing the garden."

"Ha, ha, it wouldn't hold the half of my library," Dorion told her, smiling fondly. "No, most of my business and meetings and so on will take place in my study, not the parlour, and we shall require the best room for that. You forget I will have a Duke calling on me."

"You expect me to entertain in that tiny little room?" Edith asked, surprised at his selfishness.

"Not for long. Not for long, Edith," he answered with a gloating smile; then he crept off on shuffling feet to inspect the dining room and picture to himself a Duke sitting at his board.

His stay at the Court was of indefinite duration. Edith began to fear he intended to stay there till they moved into the Vicarage and was appalled. The next day he asked Edith to go with him to the Hall, where he was eager to ingratiate himself.

"We don't visit the Hall," the Dame stated firmly.

"I know *you* don't, but this is business, Dame Durden," Dorion pointed out in his best clerical manner. "It is not a social call. You may be sure of that.

150

I share your feelings on the matter of who is socially acceptable for us to mix with."

Edith looked at him, and all the little doubts that had been festering gathered to a head in one giant ball of loathing. Hypocrite! He was delighted to have an excuse to be paying a social call on the Duke, and to deny it made it no better but a hundred times worse. Not mixing socially! Hadn't he bragged that a duke would be calling on him in the best room, specially set aside for the purpose. Hadn't he already called once to deliver his thanks, and to be taking herself along proclaimed it as a social call in the clearest manner.

"His Grace would be surprised to hear that," Edith said angrily.

Thorne looked at her in alarm. "He is not to hear it, Edith. What passes between the family is not for outsiders to hear."

"He has a good idea already," Dame Durden said with satisfaction.

When they drove up to the double doors of the Hall and were admitted by a butler, Thorne made no pretence that the visit was anything but a social one. The Duchess, however, was stunned.

"Well, if it isn't Edith Durden!" she said. "I never thought I'd see the day your mama let you come to call on me, Eddie. Come in and let us meet your young man."

Although the ladies at the Hall and the ladies at the Court did not call on each other, they, of course, met in other places and were by no means strangers. For that matter, Eddie was well acquainted with the stables and kitchens of the Hall, where she had often been with the heir during her childhood.

The Duchess turned her attention to Doctor Thorne and made him welcome as only a Doctor of Divinity could be welcomed by a religious fanatic.

"So pleased to hear you're taking over the parish, Doctor," she gushed. "A shame the way Helver let it go so long." That Helver had been abroad was either forgotten or thought too poor an excuse to proffer. "But you'll take us in hand. We've been becoming careless with only two sermons a month to tide us over. A lovely sermon you gave us Sunday. So interesting. St Paul — always one of my favourite saints. Redemption and atonement — so uplifting. I have felt the good of it all week." As it was only Monday morning, this said little for its sustaining power; but at least her heart was in the right place.

Dorion sensed at once that here was a strong ally for him. "I am happy you liked it, Your Grace," he said. "Yes, I think the positive aspects of Christianity must be emphasized. We'll leave the fire and brimstone to the Baptists."

"And the sobriety to the Methodists," she inserted, remembering her six months' commitment to that strict body.

"It is unusual to find a *lady* so keenly aware of these theoretical aspects of Christianity," he began playing up to her. She was no more interested in theology than in the theory of Copernicus, but was thrilled at the imputation.

Helver entered the room just in time to hear Thorne's last speech and glared at the sight before his eyes. "You wanted to see me, Doctor Thorne?" he asked rather impatiently.

"Your Grace!" Thorne was on his feet. "I hope I don't disturb you. Merely a social call." Edith noted the phrase and seethed. "My fiancée and I were just passing and stopped by to pay our respects."

"Very kind of you," he said and shook the outstretched hand. "I can't stay long, I'm very busy. But we'll have a glass of wine together."

The wine was produced and they all drank. Thorne found the Duke uncommunicative, and, with a meaningful glance at his bride to soften him, he returned his own attack to the Duchess. His every platitude, clothed in break-teeth words to make it unintelligible, impressed her immensely, and she felt she hadn't spent such a worthwhile half hour in months.

Helver turned aside to Edith. "It seems this wedding is to have one good effect in any case. This is the first time you have ever called on me, Eddie."

"It was Dorion's idea."

"I assumed as much. Did he have any reason for coming? Does he want to see me about something?"

"No, you heard him say it is a social call." He wondered that she should blush to admit it. She quickly went on to look about his saloon and compliment him on its various fine furnishings.

Lady Anne was still staying at the Hall, and when her Abigail heard there was company, she brushed her charge's hair and sent her belowstairs in order to give herself a rest. It was very trying playing with dolls for hours on end. Anne looked very pretty when she entered the saloon, and nodded and smiled at everyone. She liked Helver and walked to him and Edith to take a seat. She said not a word but sat down like a polite child to listen to their talk.

A few inquiries as to what she had been doing brought forth no response but only friendly smiles, and, after a moment, she picked up Edith's reticule and began looking through it.

"That's not polite, Annie," Helver chided her gently, with an apologetic smile at his guest.

"It's all right. There's nothing in it she can harm," Edith said, and Anne settled down to extract pennies and shillings and put them into neat piles, and to examine her face in a little enamelled mirror Edith carried. Doctor Thorne, informed of the girl's parentage, was eager for her acquaintance, and Anne was called away to sit with the other group.

"Poor Annie," Edith said. "It is a pity she is so retarded, for she is the prettiest little thing I ever saw."

"Oh, lord, Thorne's trying to talk religion to her," Helver said, smiling; but, to his surprise, Annie made answers to his questions. They heard in amazement that she liked church very much, with all the nice music, and with amusement that she liked to look at the ladies' hats, too.

"What will your erudite doctor make of that?" Helver asked.

"Her answer is no different from other peoples', if they told the truth."

"Yes, it's pretty hard to get the *truth* out of people. Why are you marrying him, Eddie?"

"Mama told you why."

"She told me why *she* wants you to marry him. You didn't say a word."

"My ideas are no different from hers."

"You want to marry him, then?"

"It is time I settled down."

"Dammit, Eddie, that's no reason, and you know it."

"It's a very good reason! You're trying to make something of your life; well, so am I. *I* can do something useful in the village, helping him."

"You don't have to *marry* him to be useful in the village. Who ever heard of getting married for such a reason?"

"I know you have no good opinion of marriage; I happen to feel differently."

"Well, so do I, but not about *this* marriage."

"Don't talk about it here," she said, glancing towards the other group.

"Where, then? We must talk."

"I don't know. I don't know how long he's staying. I can't go to the meadow."

"I'm coming to the Court to see you."

The Duchess arose and said to her son, "Lady Anne is going to show Doctor Thorne the garden, Helver. Why don't you and Eddie go along with them?"

The showing of the garden was not a great success. Lady Anne had the habit of pulling the petals off the prettiest roses and sprinkling them about the ground. "Snow flakes," she said, watching them sift down.

Doctor Thorne praised every bloom in view, topping his flattery by suggesting to Edith she do something of the same sort at the Vicarage after they were married. "I'm not much good at gardening," she told him unenthusiastically.

"We can't hope to match such grandeur as this, but a few bushes would smarten us up."

They did not return into the house but went from the garden to their carriage.

"Lady Anne is charming," Thorne said to Edith.

"Very pretty. A pity she's so near witless."

"I suppose she's there to make a match of it with the Duke. I wish you had told me, Edith. I like to know what is going on here."

"You must have seen her at the assembly."

"I had no idea she was making such a long visit of it. Carlton has packed her off there to marry the Duke."

"She may have come for the purpose, but Helver has no interest in her."

"She is not bright, but she is the Earl's only daughter. There will be a good dowry and that will weigh with him."

"It will not! Helver wouldn't care a fig for that."

"I notice he kept a pretty sharp eye on her when I was talking to her."

"Dorion, you can't think he was jealous!" she laughed aloud.

"As to that, if anyone were jealous in the case, it should be myself. What had His Grace to say to you?"

156

"He was only saying that this was my first formal visit to the Hall, as long as we have been neighbours."

"That was foolish of you, but, now the ice is broken, we shall go often."

Edith said not a word about social calls but only wondered at his two-facedness.

"You're certain there's to be no match between the two of them?" he asked after a few moments' silence.

"Positive. Carlton will have a hard time finding anyone to marry Anne."

The same thought had occurred to Thorne, giving rise to such a field of possibilities that he said not another word to Edith all the way home, a circumstance that pleased her.

CHAPTER
THIRTEEN

Doctor Thorne had been well pleased by his reception at the Hall. With a duchess and an earl's daughter there to lure him forth, it was his intention to return as soon and as frequently as possible. The next day, there was no mention of the call being anything but a social visit. The Dame heard with resignation of his plan. She would not go, but she did not forbid her prospective son-in-law going; neither did she urge Edith to accompany him. He felt his plans would progress more satisfactorily without her, and, as it was unlikely the Duke of Saymore would be sitting at home to be flattered into increasing his salary, Edith was not asked to accompany him.

The Duke was out on estate business, and Doctor Thorne sat with his mother, Lady Sara and Travers, urging on them his own view as to the necessity for active young clergymen in the diocese. He presented his view on heterodoxy to the Duchess's delighted ears. She felt very wise and holy, nodding her head and sipping her negus and saying he was right, quite right.

"You might tell the Dean so, next time you see him, ma'am," he remarked.

"You may be sure I will do so, Doctor," she said promptly, and didn't think to mention that she seldom saw the Dean from one year's end to the other.

Travers sat listening to his solemn patter for a while, and within a quarter of an hour figured him to be a conniver. She then excused herself, and Thorne, who mistrusted her sharp eyes, immediately enquired after Lady Anne. He was told she usually spent the mornings with her Abigail reading and was free only in the afternoons. This was carefully noted, and he timed the hour of his next visit with it in mind. It was sadly confirmed that Helver had not seemed to take to her at all, and there was to be no match in that quarter. Yes, the Duchess agreed, Carlton would have his hands full finding a husband for the girl, with her mental inadequacy. A pity, for she was really very pretty and obliging, and with a good husband she might manage a home well enough, although Carlton would have to come down heavy to find her a man.

Dorion left with his mind busy wondering what price an earl would pay to marry his daughter to an educated gentleman. When Helver returned before dinner, Travers met him on his way in.

"The Doctor's been back, buttering up your mama," she said in her blunt fashion.

"Thank God I wasn't home. Was Eddie with him?"

"No, he came alone this time."

"Why do you suppose he keeps coming here? He has the living."

"He doesn't have the Dean's position. That's what he's angling for if I read him aright."

"He aims high. What makes him think Mama can help him?"

"It never does any harm to have a duchess in your pocket."

"He's never even had a small parish of his own till now. No experience at all except for a few Sundays filling here and there when some minister was ill or on holiday. I hope he doesn't mean to hound us to death with these calls."

"Yes, strange he isn't home courting his bride-to-be. I daresay Eddie's happy enough to be rid of him for an hour a day."

"Are you hinting I should be going after Eddie? I spoke to her about this marriage. The Dame isn't pushing Thorne down her throat. She has decided to marry him."

"Have *you* decided to do nothing about it?"

"What can I do?" he asked.

"Nothing, I imagine," Travers admitted, and the two walked off in different directions but in the same dejected frame of mind.

Edith was rid of Dorion for nearly a whole day. The next morning he said he would drive over to St Michael's and talk to Mr Evans. His intention was to begin his take-over of the parish by such small steps as lending the aging Evans a hand, getting to know the people and assisting in busy periods, so that when a replacement was discussed, he would be the first name to come to mind.

Thorne made himself free with the Dame's carriage for all his outings and had the full intention of continuing to do so after he lived in the Vicarage. Wanting to set up his own was merely a pretext for more money. But he did leave Edith's mount to her. She wanted to set out for a ride, but the weather turned bad in the late morning and so she was obliged to remain indoors. Helver was caught in a cold, lashing rain on his way home, and, rather than return all the way, he sought refuge at the Court. The Dame and Eddie sat together by the huge fireplace, going through ancient tomes to discover the proper method of conducting a Tudor wedding feast.

"Now here is something," the Dame announced. "A boar's head covered with rosemary leaves. That could be done easily. I have rosemary growing in my border."

"Mama, how ghastly!" the bride objected.

"Just the head?" Helver asked. "I can't think that would feed your party. I'd prefer a joint myself."

"It is mostly ornamental, I should think," the Dame allowed. "Though a boar's cheek is not untasty. And the tongue quite unexceptionable. Now what is this — stewed goldfinches and roast porpoise? I daresay we could catch a couple of dozen finches. A pity they're all skin and bones. Cold numble pie and sack, it suggests here, for the servants."

"I'll eat with the servants," Helver said with a grimace.

"I wonder if Cook has the recipe for numble pie," the Dame asked herself. "Edith, my dear, get Helver a glass of Lamb's Wool while I speak to Cook." She crackled out of the room, and Helver looked a question at Edith.

The moment for their talk had come, and she was not anxious to begin it.

Sensing her reluctance, he said, "I hope that brew is more potable than it sounds."

"It's only March ale, with plenty of spice and sugar." She called Sally to fetch it.

"If the spice and sugar aren't yet added, you can omit them."

"They are added. We're trying out receipts for my wedding. It's quite tasty. Roasted crab-apples — only they're somewhat withered since they're last season's — and a twig of rosemary, all stirred up and foamy."

When it was brought, it resembled a meal rather than a drink, with toasted bread part of the repast. It was served hot and proved more tasty than Helver had supposed.

"Well, Eddie," he began hesitantly, "we're not likely to have a better chance than this to talk. Tell me how you came to accept him so suddenly. You said at the pavilion you hadn't made up your mind, and the next day it was all settled."

"I made up my mind, Helver. That's all." She spoke in a low voice, glancing down at her book.

"Oh, Eddie, are you going to settle for this — no romance or anything in your marriage!"

"I've decided to marry Dorion. We've told everyone. The whole village knows. He's a good man. I'm — proud to be marrying him."

Helver listened and tried to accept it. "Where is he today? He hasn't been to the Hall that I know of. Of course I haven't been home since morning."

"He's gone to visit Mr Evans," she said, and added not a single word to indicate her groom's interest in St Michael's, despite Thorne's repeated urgings that she do so.

Helver leaned back, glad to know he wouldn't be subjected to a series of "Your Graces" from Thorne. Edith was looking particularly pretty that day, with the reflections from the grate playing on her little oval face, and this unexpected visit brightening her eyes. She, too, was glad for her fiancé's absence.

"This is very nice. Homey," Helver said. It was very much like his dreams, except that Eddie was not his wife.

"We appreciate the big fireplace on days such as this."

"So you're really going to get married, Eddie. It will seem strange for you not to be here."

"I'll only be in Tisbury. I hope you mean to call on us."

"You may be sure I will. Did Thorne mention to you I'd be happy to give you away?" The phrase sounded suddenly offensive and he laughed. "Now what a thing to say! I shan't be happy in the least to give you away. What I *meant* to indicate was that as Mr Durden is dead, I'd be happy to take his part in the wedding ceremony — giving the bride away."

"I know what you meant, Helver," she said.

"You always do. How should it be possible for me to give away what is not mine?" He spoke softly and looked at her closely as he spoke. He added in a firmer voice, "And if you were mine, I wouldn't for a moment consider giving you away."

She said nothing to this but gave him such a look — full of woe — that he had for one moment a strong feeling that she was his. That look jolted him as even a direct declaration of love would not have done. There was a feeling of embarrassment between them, for Edith saw the flash of understanding leap in his eyes. "Eddie . . ." he began and made a move to arise from his seat.

"Don't!" She raised her hands in a gesture of pushing him off from her. "You forget I am engaged."

"I do not forget it," he said, resuming his seat and looking at her steadily. "And I do not understand it, either. How *could* you . . ."

"Don't say a word against him, Helver, if you wish to continue my friend." Edith didn't love Thorne, she didn't even like him; but she was engaged to marry him, and to disparage him behind his back did not seem right.

"Very well, then, but am I allowed at least a word about your own conduct?" She nodded. "It's not what I expected of you, to marry a man you don't love."

"I don't know what you did expect of me, then!" she charged angrily. "I'm nineteen years old. Did you expect me to become an old maid? To live out my life and die here at Durden Court?"

"No, I expected you to marry the man you love."

Helver didn't name the man; he didn't have to. He looked at her out of black, accusing eyes. She was so angry she felt a strong urge to slay him. Why must he

164

say this now, when it was too late? Bad enough he never made any overture of any serious sort when she was free; to come pestering her now that she was engaged was the last straw. It was also grossly improper, as she should have expected of Helver Trebourne.

"I don't love anyone," she said coldly.

"A marriage of convenience, you mean?" She didn't even bother to glance at him and gave no answer. "Perhaps you're wise after all. Maybe that's the best way. I'm thinking of settling down myself, you know."

"That will be a change."

"Now as my mentor's good wife and helpmeet, Eddie, I ask my first favour of you. Who should I marry?"

"I suggest some broad-minded lady who does not care overly much for you," she answered, anger rising in her throat.

"You think I mean to continue my amorous career after marriage? As my Vicar's wife, it is surely your duty to try to reform me. I am ready for reforming. I mean to prove some lady a good husband. I have felt, since taking over my duties, the need of a wife to come home to evenings."

"But would you come home to her? That is the question."

"If she were the right wife, I would."

"It is a Beatrice you are seeking, I assume. You never gave me the translation of that book you mentioned. You must find your own wife. I don't know what a Beatrice would be like."

"She would be like you," he said calmly and looked at her, questioning.

The Dame returned to inform them that the cold numble pie required chitterlings, and she intended to continue perusing the books for more treats. She observed nothing amiss in her companions. Helver added some light comments to her suggestions, and Edith, too, occasionally made a comment. But her mind was not on Tudor food. It was very wrong of Helver to do what he had done. To come after she was engaged to marry Dorion and try to make love to her. Very wrong, too, for her to listen to him with her heart racing. He was as bad as everyone said, and she must not listen to him. She wished he would leave — go and leave her in peace — but even after the storm abated he sat on, talking till at length Dorion returned.

"Sorry I wasn't in when you called the other day," Helver said to him. He noticed with an ironic smile that the Doctor's warm greetings were all for himself. He hardly glanced at Edith.

Thorne was gratified at the visit, most gratified, and said so a dozen times, with half a dozen "Your Graces." He went on to express his delight in the Duchess, then with the Vicarage, telling his visitor that he and Edith had been to go over it.

Edith tried to rouse herself to show some enthusiasm in her groom and her new home. "It is much finer inside than I thought," she remarked. "The bedrooms large and bright, and a closed stove in the kitchen. When did your papa have that installed?"

166

"I have no idea. Is the front room all right? It's a good-sized room, I recall. I'll redo it if you like, Eddie."

Thorne's ears perked up, and he said, "I always fancied an oak-lined study."

"But we are discussing Eddie's front room," Helver pointed out.

"Dorion will use it for a study," Eddie explained a little shamefacedly. "The study is so small — for all his books."

"I see," Helver said and dropped the subject of redoing it. "Will you take your harpsichord with you?" he asked her. "Remember you used to play that *awful* Tudor ballad on it — the one you liked so much, Dame," he said, turning to Mrs Durden.

"'The Ladye Bessie'," Eddie remembered. "Shall I play it? Would you like to hear it, Mama?"

The Dame expressed agreement with no great enthusiasm, but Doctor Thorne was loud in his request for a little music.

"We haven't played and sung together in years," Helver said to Edith. "Let's give it a try. I think I remember the words."

After a few false starts, the words and music were remembered and Dorion sat smiling, clapping at the song's end and requesting a repetition.

They played a few other songs till it was approaching dinner-time. Dorion asked Helver to remain and take potluck with them, but he eventually left.

As Helver rode home through the wet meadows, he considered the visit and was convinced on several points. Eddie didn't love Thorne, and Thorne cared for

167

no one but himself. Impossible that he had the least love for Edith, when he pushed her into intimacy with the infamous Duke of Saymore at every opportunity with the end in view of getting what he could from his wealthy patron. Eddie's scruples were overly nice, he thought, if she wouldn't listen to a word against that holy hypocrite. But how could he convince her? How could he make her believe that he had indeed changed, when she had known him for a rakehell for years? It didn't occur to him that he must make Eddie love him. She already did. Of that, at least, he hadn't the least doubt — nor of his love for her.

CHAPTER
FOURTEEN

After Helver left Thorne entertained the Durden ladies with a recital of his day at St Michael's. Evans had been happy for the few services he had been able to render and had asked him to return once a month to help out. He was also planning to set up a Sunday School for the children.

"Imagine, Edith, he doesn't have a Sunday School set up there."

"We don't have one here, either," Edith told him.

"The Saymores haven't kept an eye on things as they ought. But after we are married, you must get one going. That is woman's work."

"But you are going to do it at St Michael's?" she pointed out.

"Evans is a widower, but I'll get the parish women to do the real work. It will give a good impression for me to be able to tell His Grace my plan next time we meet. Maybe I should run over to the Hall tomorrow and mention it to him."

"I shouldn't if I were you. Helver doesn't take any interest in such things. That is — he will expect you to handle it yourself."

"The Duchess will want to hear about it," he smiled, thinking it high time to call on Her Grace again. And if he couldn't get Lady Anne involved in one way or another, he'd be much surprised.

It was his intention to go the next afternoon. In the morning he took the Dame's carriage into Tisbury to measure his study and speak to the lumber merchant about the price of oak. He forgot no detail that was to his own advantage and intended to get Eddie's present from Saymore transformed into an oak-panelled study for himself.

His trip to the Hall was delayed till after luncheon, and, upon the Doctor's arrival, Helver quickly nipped out the back door and went straight to the Court. He knew this was unconscionable behaviour, to be sneaking behind a man's back to play up to his bride-to-be, but that one look from Eddie's eyes had sent him reeling. He must convince her not to marry Thorne.

"What a pity!" she said when he was shown in. "Dorion has just gone over to the Hall to see you."

"No, it's Mama he's seeing."

"Oh, you *knew* he was there."

Dame Durden looked up sharply at this. "What exactly was it you wanted, Helver?" She had stopped suspecting his motives when he gave Dorion the living, but saw that, as she might have known, he was up to something.

He had never felt such a fool. "I wanted to *see you*," he told her.

She calmed a little at this, and he went on to explain. "It has not been quite settled I am to give your daughter away. I mentioned it to Dorion, and we agreed I should speak to you on the matter."

"I have no objection. If Edith likes it, it would be quite proper, I think. You are the lord of the village."

"I would like it," Eddie said, looking at Helver with a blank expression that told him nothing.

As his plans to see Edith alone had failed so miserably, Helver decided to leave at once, but the Dame detained him. She took him to the stables to ask his opinion of rebuilding them. Her bailiff thought it necessary, but Doctor Thorne's warning regarding the venality of bailiffs had set her to wondering. She didn't know quite how it was, but, since Dorion had come, she seemed uneasy about everything. He was quick to point a fault in all her friends and the villagers and, of course, most particularly in the Saymores. The dreadful idea was beginning to emerge that Dorion wasn't quite as fine a gentleman as she had always supposed. Dorion didn't think any work necessary in her stables, but, knowledgeable as he was in other fields, she could not but wonder when she saw wood three-quarters eaten away by rot, whether on this matter he was in error.

"You'll have the barn falling on the heads of your cattle if you don't get this set to rights," Helver told her at a glance.

She then asked him several questions about the milking sheds at the Hall, which she had heard to be in a state of renovation, with some modern improvements she was interested in. The house must remain a Tudor museum, but she was not so insane on the matter that she scorned modern methods in her work areas. This took a long time, for Helver was enthusiastic and, by now, well informed about such agricultural affairs. They examined the stables, and, when they returned to the house chilled from their outing, a warm drink seemed to be in order. Doctor Thorne returned before Helver left and felt himself doubly blessed to have had the Duchess's ear to himself and the honour of a call from His Grace. That he had also managed a fifteen minutes' stroll with Lady Anne through the Saymore rose garden, telling her how much fun she would have at his little Sunday School with pretty Edith reading her stories, added to his high spirits. His Grace must not think of leaving till he had been informed of the Sunday School. Dame Durden, having already heard of her and Edith's duties in that regard, departed with a crackle of her stiff skirts to have the stables measured.

"Not a bad notion," was Helver's bland comment. "But I don't think memorizing the Bible and that sort of thing much use." "*These be the words which Moses spake unto all Israel*" — the old familiar, meaningless phrases from Deuteronomy surfaced in his mind.

"That will be up to my wife," Thorne replied. "Edith has been kind enough to offer to undertake setting up the school. A good pastime for a vicar's wife, I think you will agree, Your Grace."

Helver smiled to see Eddie's discomfort in her new role. "In that case, there is no fear of an overdose of memorizing. Have you learned the alphabet yet, Eddie?"

"Oh, yes. You are reverting far into the past to remember my difficulty with it. In fact, I was only five when I had the alphabet off by heart."

"You were at least six, my girl. I was either eleven or twelve, for I remember I had my tutor — young Hackett — copy it out for you, with an animal or something for every letter. Hackett didn't come to us till I was eleven."

"I don't remember," Edith lied blandly, yet she still remembered aardvark, bat, cat, dog as well as if it were yesterday.

"Your friendship with each other goes back a long way," Dorion said.

"Your fiancée has a shockingly bad memory, Doctor. Did you know that?" Helver asked, with a teasing smile at Eddie.

"As long as she remembers she is a minister's wife, I think we may count on her good sense not to lead her astray."

"I daresay she won't be forgetting that."

"Perhaps you two would like to be alone," Edith said, acutely aware that Helver was bent on mischief and in an excellent position to perpetrate it, knowing her so much better than did Thorne.

"No, stay, my dear," Thorne said. It was the first time he had ever called her by such an endearment. "You and the Duke are old friends." Edith looked in vain for an edge of irony in this. Finding none, she remained seated.

"We have been friends from the cradle," Helver told him. "Almost like brother and sister, in fact."

Thorne smiled warmly at this, always happy to see the closeness of Edith to the Duke. "A wonderful thing, friendship," he began to preach. "I hope your friendship will not flag only because your sister," he smiled at Edith, "is about to be married. Indeed, I hope that in time, Your Grace, you will come to regard me as something of a brother." Having failed as a father, he was willing to go for the next best thing. "An older brother; one who is always willing to give his help, advice, when they may be needed. My door will always be open to you."

"You have mentioned before your willingness to guide me, Doctor Thorne. I shall bear it in mind if I find myself in need of such help."

It was settled that Helver was to give the bride away, after which interlude Helver tried to leave but was detained by the Doctor. "Might I trouble you, Your Grace, for another rendition of that delightful ballad you and Edith were so kind as to sing for us the other day? 'The Ladye Bessie,' I think it was called."

Edith's anger with Helver began to shift to Thorne. If Helver had come to make mischief, Dorion was only too eager to egg him on to it. He always did everything in his power to encourage the friendship between them, and she decided she must show him a lesson. She would be as friendly with Helver as even her groom-to-be could wish and perhaps his eyes would be opened. "Very well. I always like singing with Helver," she said, and gave him, to his great surprise, a sweet smile. So sweet, in fact, that he looked automatically to Dorion for some signs of offence but found none.

They sang the song and again, as on the day before, an encore was not only asked but demanded. "Let's sing something else," Helver said. "There was always a ton of music in that old parson's bench in the hall."

"We don't have a parson's bench in the hall," Edith advised him.

"You used to. Don't you remember the time we were sliding down the bannister and you cracked your head against the back of it?"

"My arm, you mean. I couldn't move my elbow for a week, and you gave me horse liniment for it. But I don't know what bench you mean. It was an old chest there."

"Yes, so it was. I remember it now — with brass corners and leather straps around it."

"It's in the study, with a potted fern on it."

It was dragged out, and its contents called up more shared memories from the past, each of which was gone into with readiness by Edith, with frequent little peeps at Dorion for signs of disapproval. So far from disapproving, he sat nodding benignly on her while she flirted with the most handsome, dashing, reckless blade in the kingdom. Thorne urged them to reminisce, inserting the words "brother" and "sister" from time to time, though he must surely have seen that no such relationship now existed between them. When they returned to the instrument to sing "Blowzie Bella," he excused himself for a moment.

For one song they thought nothing of his absence, but after two they began to look at each other questioningly. "What can be keeping Dorion?" Edith asked.

"Maybe he doesn't care for our music."

"He asked us to play."

"So he did."

Edith felt guilty after her performance and said rather penitently, "I daresay he disliked our talking so freely of the past."

"Oh, no, he liked that. He even seemed amused at your flirting. What are you trying to do, make him jealous?"

"I wasn't flirting."

"Well, whatever you were doing, I wouldn't like *my* fiancée to do it with another man. He's always throwing you at my head. Serves him right. Come on, we'll find a nice warm love ballad and see if that brings him back. How about . . ."

"He is not doing *that*!" she charged angrily.

"Isn't he? You wouldn't be left alone with another man if you were engaged to *me*."

"Well, I'm not engaged to you."

"I know," he said curtly, "but it's damned odd your lover doesn't show any signs of jealousy when you're acting almost as though you were."

"Dorion is above jealousy."

"Then he isn't human!"

"Don't you dare call him a *snake* again, Helver. *We're* the snakes, both of us."

"We're not doing anything. But we could be. I could be making violent love to you for all he knows. Why doesn't he look after you?"

"He has a better opinion of you than that, and of me, I hope." Whatever about herself, she knew in her heart Dorion's opinion of Helver was not high, and why didn't he come back?

"He has no high opinion of anyone except possibly himself. Very much aware of human failings; he's said so more than once."

"You told him we were like brother and sister. Why should he be jealous? He only wants us to remain friends."

"Why the deuce should he want that? He's got the living — unless I am expected to confer further honours, or salary, for the privilege of making free with his wife."

"How dare you say such a thing! Only you would place such a construction as that on his trusting actions. You speak as though — oh, Helver, I'm ashamed of you!"

As angry as she was with her fiancé, she couldn't believe him capable of any such villainy as Helver had mentioned. Mama was right, and Helver was a deep-dyed villain. How could such an idea have occurred to him?

Helver felt somewhat ashamed of himself when he saw the shocked look on Eddie's face.

After allowing what he considered sufficient time for Helver to have been softened by love songs, Doctor Thorne returned to mention Evans's creeping infirmity, ever so casually, and hint that it was getting on to time to think of retiring him. But the subtle words died on his lips. He saw the two staring at each other, obviously in the middle of a fight.

"What, a family squabble?" he asked, with one fast, fierce look directed at Edith. "What will His Grace think of you, my dear?"

"His Grace is about to leave," she said.

"Doctor Thorne stands on the formality of calling me so, Eddie, but *we*, I hope, are on a closer footing than that." Helver said. "I hope you don't mean to sink me to 'Your Grace,' only because you are about to become a vicar's *wife*."

"If her memory is so feeble, I must call you Helver, too." Thorne suggested playfully.

"Why not, Dorion?" Helver asked, smiling sardonically. "After all, we are all about to become one big happy family."

"Quite so. Quite so. All one happy family, and we must not leave out Her Grace."

"Let's add Dame Durden for good measure," Helver added and strode to the door.

"I hope you don't leave us in anger, Helver," Thorne said, walking rapidly after him.

"Not in the least. I plan to do myself the honour of returning tomorrow. We families must keep the ties close."

"Indeed, we must," Thorne agreed, holding the door for the Duke. Immediately Helver had left, he turned in wrath on his bride. "Fool! What did you say to upset him?"

"You should be asking what *he* said to upset *me*! *I* should be your first consideration," she shot back, furious with both of them.

"My first consideration is not to lose His Lordship's regard. He can do us a world of good if we play our cards right."

"What is our trump card, Dorion? Me? Am *I* the queen of hearts?"

"Ha! Ha! Very sharp. He has a keen regard for you. You did well to play up to him a little. You are something more than a sister to him, I think. That can be turned to good account. Oh, not that any impropriety must arise! Scandal and gossip would be worse than anything for my career. A woman's smiles, however, can accomplish a good deal in this world. Especially with men of Saymore's kidney. And mind it is to go no further than *smiles*."

"Saymore is not the sort to be satisfied with smiles," she told him and marched angrily from the room. She went upstairs to consider the vileness of the world. She was shocked at Helver's idea that Dorion would use her to advance himself, but more shocked that it was true. Helver was an acknowledged rakeshame and that he would come up with such an idea shouldn't shock her, but it did. And how could she come to terms with Dorion's suggestion of going along with it? Was he so blind, so trusting and basically innocent as to think any man would demand no more than a smile for conferring large favours? She regretted deeply that she had ever allowed herself to be talked into this marriage. She had accepted it half to avoid being hurt by Helver, and now it seemed that was to be thrown into the bargain. She argued with herself whether she could call off the wedding and how it could be done. Thorne

179

would be adamant, and it would require Mama's support.

She remained in her room through dinner, claiming a headache. Her mother came to her later; and, to give her a hint of the way things were going, she said, "I cannot like Dorion's scheming to get himself into Helver's good graces, Mama."

The Dame had a good inkling this was going on, for Dorion spoke quite openly in the family. "It is a pity he is in a position where he has to do so. A great pity for one of his superior breeding to have to stoop to his inferiors, but the world is hard. Dorion must behave now in a way we none of us like, for the sake of his future. That young man is going far, Edith, and you at his side."

Edith felt her position was more in advance than at his side and frowned. "I don't think it is proper for Helver to be here so much. It gives an odd appearance."

"Dorion is broad-minded. He doesn't mind about that. He is above jealousy. For myself, I do mistrust Helver's motives. His coming here when he knew Dorion to be at the Hall was ill-done. But we know what he is. His past is not such that it leaves any doubt. A series of entanglements with females of all sorts — he has no character. None at all; and, if he comes again, I think you must be busy, Edith."

"I think I must; but it is Dorion who ought to have said so, not us."

"It would not occur to him to suspect such treachery. He places too much reliance on the title. In that one

180

small matter I do think he is out in his judgement. To see him trotting over to the Hall to make up to Dora Trebourne is not what I ever expected of him."

"I have been unhappy with his behaviour ever since Helver returned. I must confess, Mama, I have doubts about marrying him."

"I know you have, my dear," her mother said quietly. "Helver has gone out of his way to turn your head, but it is pure mischief. *He* has no more thought of marrying you himself than he would marry any of the other scores of girls in this county he has ruined. I hope you are not so simple-minded as to hope for that, love. His blood lines quite aside, he is too high for us. Gentlemen in his walk of life, aristocracy as they consider themselves, do not marry such as you. And if it's a title you want, well, a bishop is also a lordship, you know."

"Helver is not — I don't think he's quite as bad as he's made out," Edith defended, but her defence was weak after his afternoon's work.

"I have taken care that the reports of his more infamous conduct do not reach your ears. There is no reason for young ladies to hear such tales. Enough that you know he is not respectable."

"I am no longer a *young* lady. I am about to be married, and surely I can know the whole now."

"What you suspect he has in mind in coming here — to turn you away from a good marriage for a brief flirtation — is the sort of thing he does regularly. A dozen times Dora Trebourne has lamented to me of his conduct when visiting relatives; and, if his own mother

181

cannot turn a blind eye to his conduct, it would be madness for you to do so. You made the right decision to marry Dorion and forget Helver. Don't be turned aside from it by his flashing eyes or you'll regret it the rest of your life, Edith."

So even Mama was not totally unaware of the danger in those flashing eyes. Edith smiled when her mama thought she ought to be serious and repeated her warnings at more length before leaving her daughter with a headache somewhat increased, and a heavy heart. Very likely Mama was right — but what if she wasn't? What if Helver was truly bent on reforming, as he said he was, and what if he loved her as he hadn't any of those other scores of girls? Then, too, while Dorion might have to truckle a little to Saymore to ingratiate him, he did not have to encourage herself to play up to him. That was ill-done of him; but it was innocent folly, being unaware of the way it would be interpreted by a man such as Helver. Nothing was settled in her mind. The disgrace of jilting Thorne was a considerable barrier to that course, made worse by her mother's wanting the marriage so much. Had she been privy to the Dame's deepest feelings, she might have felt differently; for, while the Dame still wanted the wedding, still saw a danger in Helver, she was less enthusiastic about Dorion than formerly. The Dame lay awake a long while considering the same problem. The greatest pity of it all was that she liked Helver very much despite his terrible reputation. When he sat with her, joking good-humouredly and talking up her May Day revels and so on, she really felt that she would like him very much for a son-in-law. He had been very helpful in the business of the stables, too. Was coming to know a good deal about farming, which was a thing she had not expected in him. Like her daughter, she counted up the days till the marriage and half hoped something would occur to alter the present plans.

Across the meadows in the Hall, the Duke of Saymore was racking his brain to think how he could change the plans that were afoot. He meant to have Eddie for himself if he must snatch her away from the altar with a brace of pistols to do so, but he preferred for her to come to him willingly. And for this her precious Doctor Thorne must be exposed for the scheming, conniving rascal he was. A dozen ideas darted into his head. An outright cash sum, if large enough, would do the trick, he fancied, or a better — *much* better — post elsewhere. But this would have to be done privately between himself and Thorne, and what he really wanted was for Eddie to come to see the true nature of this man she spoke so highly of.

CHAPTER
FIFTEEN

Between visits to Durden Court by the Duke of Saymore and visits to the Hall by the Doctor, the two families were on more intimate terms than they had formerly enjoyed. Doctor Thorne now made quite a habit of running over to the Hall every day and was always made welcome by the Duchess, and Lady Anne as well, as he timed his calls for the afternoon, when she would be free. He told her simple stories from the Bible and helped her pick roses to pull apart and, bit by bit, began to slide in compliments on her pretty blue eyes and golden hair. When they were well beyond earshot of others, he called her a pretty little angel and said he would like to adopt her and take her home with him. She laughed in mindless delight and called him a funny old man, pointing at his bits of grey hair. He was not in the least offended, for he thought she was coming to like the funny old man. She ran to meet him now when he called. Thorne was busy playing two hands of cards at the same time. He was engaged to Edith and thought he might very well marry her, but he continued to encourage Helver to call and befriend her. This now had a two-fold purpose. If he married her, she would have Helver wrapped around her finger to advance his progress; and, if events fell out in such a way that it seemed possible Carlton might listen to his suit, he could throw in Edith's face that she was unworthy of being a vicar's wife when she had been openly dangling after Saymore ever since becoming engaged. With this alternative in view, he occasionally got on his high ropes with her in private, but, when Saymore was present, he was all smiling compliance.

Edith's head was spinning. Just when she became convinced Dorion was using her to win Saymore, he would light into her and make her feel guilty. And through it all, Helver kept coming to the Court, flirting with her, reminding her of the old days and occasionally calling her "dear sister." The Dame suggested to Dorion that he hint Helver away, but he wouldn't hear of it; he laughed and spoke of one big happy family. There was an uneasy atmosphere heavy about the place, charged with emotion, and it seemed some spark must ignite an explosion before the wedding date came around.

On one of his many visits to the Hall, Thorne felt himself enough at home to tell the butler he needn't announce him. He walked into the Gold Saloon and found Lady Sara sitting with Anne, stringing large papier-mâché beads on a thread. Both were happy to see the Doctor for their different reasons. Lady Sara saw an excellent opportunity to gain a respite from the trying Lady Anne and promptly suggested she take Thorne out to the garden for a little walk. He offered her his arm and off they went together, the learned doctor and the moonling, to pull off roses and play snow flakes. She shredded two or three, laughing gaily as the petals drifted to the ground. Then she pulled a red rose off its stock and handed it to Dorion to play with. He took the rose and stuck it in his buttonhole. "I shall keep it to remind me of you," he said with a gallant bow. She promptly pulled off another and handed it to him.

"You keep this one, to remind you of me," he said.

She smiled agreeably and stuck it into her bosom, then reached out for his hand and pulled him along to a fountain. "Fish!" she said, pointing to ornamental goldfish gliding about a small pond by the fountain.

"Yes, see the pretty fish," he said. "Does Annie like swimming?"

She shook her head in a negative and settled down to the watching of the fish. With a confiding smile, she put her hand in his and the mismated pair sat silently watching the fish swim.

"Does Annie have fish at home?" he plodded on with his courting.

She didn't give any answer to this. "Is Annie's papa good to her?" he asked next, and this got a nodding smile of affirmation.

"Does Papa let her have whatever she wants?" he asked leadingly.

Hardly knowing what he meant, she nodded again, still looking at the fish. "Does Annie want Doctor Thorne?" he asked with a little careful glance towards the house to ensure their privacy. She laughed and frowned at the same time, casting a truly witless look on her pretty face. It thrilled him. Carlton would never get a husband for the girl. He should be delighted that an educated gentleman like himself was interested.

"Would Annie like to have Doctor Thorne to keep?" he asked.

"Annie keep Doctor," she said, squeezing his hand a little harder.

"You must tell your papa you want Doctor Thorne," he said. "Can you remember that, Annie?"

She seemed to have forgotten it already. She pulled a head of clover from the grass and threw it into the pond to attract a fish to the surface.

It was thus they were discovered a moment later by Lord Carlton when he stopped off at the Hall on his way home from a business call that had brought him to Tisbury. He had come to see how it was going on with Anne and Saymore; and Lady Sara had directed him to the rose garden, where his surprise was great to see his little daughter arm-in-arm with an elderly gentleman, with no sign of a chaperone. When he recognized who the gentleman was, his face stiffened into disapproval, for he had some knowledge of Thorne.

Dorion got around a good bit replacing ministers on a temporary basis. He had last year been for over a month at Bath, not far from Carlton's place, and what Lord Carlton knew of the fellow he did not like. He was highly displeased to see Annie so unprotected but could not like to create a fuss with the Duchess. He formed the strict resolution to take her home with him that day.

He chose his words carefully, but his tone left Thorne in no doubt as to the father's feelings. "So, Annie, I see you are entertaining Doctor Thorne."

She smiled and ran to her father. "See the fish swim!" she said, pulling him along to the pond.

Carlton looked at the rose in her gown and at the rose in Thorne's lapel and said, "Have you been a naughty girl, picking the Duchess's flowers?"

"Doctor gave me," she said, touching her rose.

Thorne was ready to slap her. "What a charming daughter you have, Lord Carlton," Dorion began playing up to him.

"I am very fond of little Annie. I wonder she is left alone to wander about the grounds with a gentleman."

"Annie likes the Doctor," the girl said. "Can I keep him?"

"She was showing me the roses," Thorne said, trying to make it sound as though he had been minding her, like a nanny.

"Very kind of you, I'm sure," Lord Carlton replied icily, and, tucking Annie's hand into his arm, he left without another word.

It was one thing to see Annie marry the Duke of Saymore and quite another to see her and that queer nabs of a Thorne sitting with their heads together. Whisk her off home at once.

Say she was homesick. But first he was desirous of discovering how it had progressed between her and the man with whom she had come to attach herself, and he asked for an interview with Saymore.

He had to wait a little for his return, and, when Helver did come, he suspected nothing amiss. Thorne had deemed it wisest to go back to Durden Court without returning to the house, so Helver did not know of the visit. The men shook hands and Carlton asked bluntly, "Well, Saymore, how did it go?"

"With Lady Anne? Why, we enjoyed having her. She is delightful. Quite charming."

"Yes, yes, but between you two?"

"Well, she is very lovely, but . . ."

"Not bright. There's no pretending she's bright. So you ain't interested, then?"

"Not in marriage, Sir. I regret if that is the impression you were given."

"Cut line, Saymore. It was all the Duchess's doings. I didn't think you'd take to Annie. And she ain't the right wife for a gentleman like yourself, either. Still, she's a good girl and a pretty little thing. The thing is, if you ain't interested, I'll just take her on home with me. Save me a trip back, and we miss her."

"Perhaps she would be better amused at home."

"We're used to her ways. It's not so bad, having a little girl that never grows up. We love Annie very much."

"I'm sure you do, Sir."

"Not that I think you weren't taking good care of her, but I don't like that Thorne was alone with her in the garden just now."

"Oh, lord, is that bleater here again?" Helver asked impatiently.

"Aye, sitting holding hands with Annie when I saw them in the garden. Been making up to her, I believe. The Duchess can't know about him."

"Know what about him?" the Duke demanded, instantly alert.

"Not quite the thing, that fellow. I should have thought *you'd* have heard . . ."

"I know nothing to his discredit. I wish you will tell me. I've just made him Vicar of Tisbury."

"Made him Vicar? Dear me, what were you thinking of?"

"He is highly thought of here. Pray, tell me what he's done."

"He didn't do anything actually, but it's discussed quite openly around Bath that he was trying to get Sir Harold Cuthbertson's girl to run off with him. Rich as a nabob, you know, old Cuthbertson, and Sally the only child. A pretty little wench of eighteen but a bold hussy. No doubt you know *her*."

"No, she must have been quite young when I left on my trip. And you're telling me she and Thorne planned a runaway match?"

"As much the chit's doings as his, I daresay. He goes about with that holy face and religious patter that gulls all the mamas into thinking him a saint. He had a group of the young girls in helping him run some sort of a Sunday School, and before long Sally Cuthbertson was staying after classes, making up to the Doctor. But I don't hold him innocent in the matter. She was only a silly young girl, but he's old enough to know better. He led her on, no doubt of that. They planned to run off; but the girl told some friend or other, and the story got back to her parents in time to prevent it. Cuthbertson would never have given his approval to the match, of course. They look higher than a penniless cleric for Sally. The Cuthbertsons hushed it up as well as they could, but with the friend telling a friend and so on, it is generally known. A pity you've made him your Vicar, but there are no heiresses here for you to worry about."

"He was holding hands with Annie in the garden just now, you say? I owe you a great apology, Carlton. I had no idea this was going on. Thorne is considered above reproach here. I can at least assure you he has not been beyond the garden with Annie. He calls regularly on Mama, and he and Annie seem to hit it off."

"He'd see to that! Had given her a rose to stick in her dress, the demmed jackanapes, and he with another."

"Oh, God — but were they just holding hands?"

"Yes, yes, nothing to get in a pucker over — don't bother the Duchess with the story. I'll be taking her on home, however, as there's nothing between you."

"Certainly, and you may be sure I'll speak to Thorne."

"As to that, not much you can say. He was only sitting with her, watching the fish. Not much you can accuse him of, but he bears watching. I'd keep a sharp eye on him."

"I'll watch him like a hawk. I have reasons of my own for disliking the man."

"What the devil did you make him your Vicar for, then?"

"He's marrying my neighbour, Miss Durden, and needed the living."

"What, marrying the Durden girl? I hadn't heard that. The Dame might have done better for her daughter — but then, she's a little odd about genealogy, ain't she?"

"She's quite eccentric, but there will be no match now."

"Has he called off? It'll be my Annie he's got ideas about."

"No, he hasn't called off, but she shall."

"She's a good catch for Thorne. Must have a good dowry, the only child. He'll not let her off once I get Annie packed off out of here. If you've made him your Vicar, you'd do better to let the match go on. A wife will keep him on the straight and narrow, and, if the wife don't, the Dame will. A whim of iron, as they say."

"No, he shan't marry her now. Not now that I know this," Helver said in a voice of quiet conviction.

Carlton regarded him narrowly. "You seem mighty interested, Saymore."

"I am, *mighty* interested."

"I heard mentioned somewhere you and the De Courcy widow were hitting it off. Nothing came of that?"

"No, no — that was nothing serious."

"Glad to hear it. You could do better than De Courcy's leavings. But you're thinking of taking a wife, are you?"

"I think of it a great deal lately."

"Glad to hear it. We — men in our position, I mean — need a woman to take care of us. Your racketing days are over, eh, Saymore? Well, choose wisely. It's one of the most important decisions you'll ever have to make. The wrong woman can be the ruination of a man. I was troubled when I heard about you and the De Courcy woman. I thought of riding over and having a chat with you, but we've never been close; and with Annie here it looked as though I was trying to bring pressure to bear. Your father and I were friends, but there's a lot of years between us. I'm sorry the old Duke is gone. I see there are changes taking place. A group of new cottages going up along the river. Look very nice."

"Yes, I have plenty to do."

"You would have. The young have their own ideas. I'm happy to see you settling down. It's no sinecure, whatever others may think. You always know where I am if you want a grey head to talk a problem over with. I wish I were closer."

The command was given for Annie's belongings to be packed, and the gentlemen went to the study to discuss farming, politics and the many aspects of their lives over a bottle of claret. When Annie was brought down, her father took her hand, smiled a little sadly at Saymore, whom he considered would have made Annie a very good husband, and took his leave. The Duchess forgot why Annie had come to them and what a nuisance she had been, and expressed the desire that she return again very soon.

"We'll see," the Earl said with a knowing look at Helver, and left.

Helver strolled out into the garden. He had much to think about. The fallen petals on the ground reminded him of Annie, and he was furious at Thorne's trying to make up to the girl. She was pretty, of course, but so simple that Thorne's being after her could have only one explanation. He wanted to make the most advantageous marriage possible — and all this going forth while his marriage to Eddie was less than a month away. This and his past affair with Miss Cuthbertson removed any last shred of doubt as to his much-praised character. The man was a thoroughgoing scoundrel who would stoop to any trick to advance himself in the world. Having lost out on Lady Anne, he would surely marry Eddie if he didn't stop him. He was absolutely determined to prevent the match.

But how to discredit him? Eddie didn't love him, but she clearly admired him and would listen to no stories of his carrying on. It would be interpreted as an invention of his own and only serve to lower himself in her eyes. How she had stared at him the other day when he pointed out what Dorion was up to, throwing them together. She hadn't believed a word of it. Helver wondered if it had been Thorne's intention to be rid of Eddie to marry Anne and to use himself as an excuse. Perhaps that was it and not what he had suspected all along, that Eddie was being used to weasel favours out of an influential duke. Either way, it was no credit to the Doctor. As he considered the past weeks, he thought Dorion had been encouraging the friendship between Edith and himself before he got to chasing after Annie. It was as he had first thought; and how far would Dorion be willing to go? Helver's heart thudded with the idea of carrying it to its extremity — to offer outright to get him some high post in exchange for an affair with his wife. It was risky. Supposing Thorne stopped short of outright bartering for Edith? Where was he then? Disgraced, for good and all. With his reputation no one would believe it had been only a trick. And, even if Thorne accepted the idea, how was Eddie to be made to believe it? It couldn't be done before her very face, yet that was the only way she'd believe it of Thorne. "He is above jealousy," she had said. He was above nothing, including marrying a half-wit for the sake of her family connections, and her dowry.

Thorne's own mind was busy as he returned to the Court. Old Carlton had seen right through him, and he hadn't liked it a bit. Should have been flattered that a grown man, and an educated one, would condescend to sit with that witless girl and watch her tear flowers to bits. Very likely he had heard about Sally Cuthbertson. He had thought the matter was hushed up, but likely every father with a marriageable daughter was in on it. It was more imperative than ever that he marry Edith now. He had lost Anne, but she had never been more than a distant possibility. Thorne's real concern was that Carlton would tell Saymore the whole history of the Bath episode. Saymore was very fond of Edith. God only knew what he would do if he ever learned the truth. Have to tell the Dame Saymore was jealous of him, to prepare her in case the story came out. He'd say it was all a lie, and the Dame would believe his story — a Doctor and a minister of the Church of England — above Saymore's. The fellow really acted damnedly jealous at times. The fact was he was hankering after Edith himself. A fool could see as much. But, of course, he'd never marry her. A duke might marry anyone he chose and wouldn't be likely to choose a prissy little armiger's daughter. Still, he was plenty jealous of the man who would marry her and might well use the Sally Cuthbertson affair to break the match if he could. It might even have some bearing on the Tisbury living! He'd have to tred softly with Saymore, and, thank God, he had the Duchess and Lady Sara in his pocket.

He went out of his way to be amiable to Edith and her mama that evening to make them think better of him. "What's new at the Hall?" Edith asked the old familiar question.

"I stayed only a moment. Lord Carlton had come to call, and I didn't stay. It is a great pity, that daughter of his. I took her into the garden to try to gauge the extent of her condition. I fear she is hopelessly simple. Quite a child, pulling flowers apart and watching the fish play. A very child — a sweet, innocent child."

"It is a great pity. Did you see Saymore?"

"We are to call him Helver, my dear. No, I didn't see him. I don't like to bother him with my small problems. You and I shall manage our affairs at the Vicarage, and very happy we shall be doing it."

"And very busy."

"That is true. There are half a dozen christenings and a few marriages. I don't think I'll ask you to press that matter of St Michael's just for the present. One thing at a time. There is much to be done here, and I have my writing, too. The Theological Society has asked me to prepare an article for publication in their journal.

196

My thesis on heterodoxy is to be compressed into a few thousand words for the next quarterly."

The aspect of marriage with Dorion that most pleased Edith was that it would put her into the middle of village life. So cut off and lonesome as she had been, she did look forward to that with some pleasure. To hear him speak of christenings and marriages and know that she would be present almost made her think she could be happy as Mrs Thorne. Helver had been acting so badly of late, coming daily to pester her and flirt with her, that she saw no possibility of his settling into a suitable mate. Dorion's talk of his writing, too, made her aware of his mental superiority to not only herself but most of the village. She softened to the extent of smiling at him, and he relaxed almost visibly.

"I'm glad you've given up the idea of St Michael's, Dorion. It is really too much to ask."

He noted her approval and was quick to follow this lead up. "It was conceited of me to think *I* could tend to their spiritual needs more than another. I shall undertake to give a hand to the chap who gets it, though."

"That would be nice of you."

"Then there is the Duke of Saymore, whom I shall endeavour to help out in his private affairs." Edith looked her disagreement with this. "Don't scold me, Edith. I like him very much, but it is no secret he is — well, not so fine an example as he could be to his people. Why, even his behaviour to you is not quite what one could wish at times. We shall show him the true happiness to be found in the married state and try

197

to bring him around to more proper behaviour. I mean by example only. I shan't preach to him. I know he dislikes that."

"Yes, he does."

"And we shan't forget your mother, either. She must come often to visit us, and we shall come here, too, of course."

He talked on in this happy vein till Edith was half convinced he wasn't as bad as she thought. She could find happiness, leading a useful life among the villagers, with an admired and respected husband. If only Dorion would give up once and for all the idea of taking over another parish, she could find some measure of contentment. Unlike her fiancé, she did not look forward to the visits from Helver with anything but dread, especially if they were to take the personal, intimate trend they had been taking. But she could manage that. Tell Helver outright he must not come too often. Dorion would hate it if he ever found out, but scandal must be avoided; and, if her husband was too much locked up in his ivory tower to see the danger, it was her duty to circumvent it.

The Dame, Dorion and herself spent a quiet evening together in a happier state than they had done before. As Helver did not come pouncing down from the Hall to call Thorne to account, he assumed he had escaped free from Carlton's visit.

CHAPTER
SIXTEEN

Helver knew the step he was considering to be a dangerous one and mulled it over in his mind that evening and the next day as he made his rounds with Forringer. He left an hour earlier than usual in the afternoon, returned to the Hall and dressed himself in visiting clothes to call at the Court. In his jacket of blue Bath cloth, biscuit-coloured trousers and his shiny Hessians, he was an impressive sight.

"Such a determined face in such handsome dress! You look very much like a man with a purpose," Travers joked him as he walked to the door. He looked a shade paler today, too.

"I have somewhere to go," he replied stiffly.

Travers was a little worried to hear this. "Where?" she asked.

"To the Durdens'."

"Oh. Doctor Thorne is still there, is he?"

"I hope so. It is Thorne I have to see."

Travers's worries mounted to alarm. Alone of his family she knew there had been something troubling him lately. She had noticed his antipathy to Thorne and suspected its cause. Her whole desire was that he marry Edith, yet she did not wish to see him do anything foolish or downright wrong. She didn't think he had rigged himself out in good clothes to impress Thorne.

"Be careful," she warned.

"I am walking on eggs, Travers. Keep your fingers crossed fot me."

"What is it, Helver? Tell me; it helps to talk things over with a cool, old head."

"You wouldn't approve. I'm not sure I approve myself, but it must be done."

"Helver, don't . . ."

"Not to worry. I'll be back soon, one way or the other."

"It isn't a duel!" she gasped. The "one way or the other" had a suggestion of "dead or alive" about it due to the grim tone in which it had been uttered.

"Well," he considered it a moment, "not a duel with pistols. A battle of wits, shall we say?"

"Oh, well in that case you're safe," she said, breathing easier. "Though Thorne is a cunning rascal — up to any trick."

"Up to a few that surprised even me, and I thought I was the shadiest gent in the village." With a wave and even an effort at a smile, he was off. Travers went up to her room and prayed for half an hour.

Helver found Edith and Thorne together in the living room, writing a list of guests for the wedding. The Dame was busy in the stables, poking her fingers into rotting wood and estimating the cost of replacing it.

"Your Grace," Thorne said, jumping up to make him welcome with a handshake. He looked warily at Helver, trying to read his mood. He remarked the careful toilette and wondered what could account for it. Helver usually called in his working clothes, but he knew this afternoon was to be a turning point in his life and had honoured it in this fashion, perhaps with a view to making himself more attractive to Edith. Its effect was rather otherwise; she assumed he had taken such pains because he was off to chase some new flirt. She schooled herself to prefer Dorion's plain black suit and not to compare their walks as they both came into the room.

"Edith and I were just making out our list of wedding guests," Thorne ran on nervously. "You will see the Duchess's name leads all the rest. I have convinced the Dame that for this special occasion past enmities must be forgotten. It will be a first visit for your mother, I believe."

"It will be a first invitation," Helver answered, taking a seat between Edith and Thorne. He noticed they had been sitting on separate seats, Edith on the settee, Thorne on a chair. There wasn't a loverlike instinct in the man's whole body.

"It will not be a last," Dorion said. "I hope we may continue on sociable terms with the Hall after the marriage."

"How is your mother?" Edith asked.

"Fine. A little lonely. Carlton came yesterday and took Annie home."

"Dorion said he was there but didn't say Annie was leaving."

"For some reason, Carlton was anxious to get her home at once," Helver said, with a hard stare at Dorion that sent the Doctor to inward trembling.

So the news was out. "That child must be a trial to him," Dorion said, quick to establish his innocence. "I was walking about the garden with her to relieve your Aunt Sara of the burden and was very impressed with her childishness. I hadn't been much alone with her before and hadn't quite realized the extent of her condition. It is very sad."

"Yes, for in her position she might easily be taken advantage of. They must exercise the greatest vigilance to protect her. She is not wise enough to realize the danger inherent in fortune hunters and will take up with anyone who is kind to her."

"No gentleman would consider her a possible bride!" Edith said. Helver and Dorion exchanged a speaking glance.

"One would think her condition would protect her — and so it would, from a *gentleman*," Helver replied.

"Certainly," Dorion added firmly.

"So, Dorion," Helver turned to face Thorne head on. "You are thinking of moving into the Vicarage? You will want a little work done there before you move your bride in."

"You did mention redoing my study," Thorne replied, happy to see the Lady Anne fracas pass from consideration. He assumed this was to be the end of it. A gentle, indirect hint that it was known, and a tacit warning about such carryings on. "I happened to notice some nice oak lumber at . . ."

"You misunderstood me," Helver corrected. "It was Eddie's saloon I wished to redecorate for her. Decide what you want done to it, Eddie — anything within reason. Or for you, beyond reason. Would you like some chandeliers, a marble fireplace, new carpets . . .”

Thorne's eyes bulged, but Edith pokered up at once. “I think such refinements would look out of place in a vicarage. The room is well enough as it is.”

“Not good enough for you, Eddie. Like your husband, I want the best for you.”

“It is a trifle small,” Thorne began, foreseeing a whole new addition to the house.

“Indeed, it is,” Helver agreed, with a wicked light coming to his eyes. “As this selfish fellow,” he laughed to show he joked, “has taken over your saloon, I think I must rebuild you a new one.”

Edith noticed Helver's satirical face and frowned heavily. “If you insist on spending money on us, do as Dorion wishes with his study.”

“But I want to do something for *you*. Dorion understands my feelings,” Helver said and knew from the avaricious, calculating expression on Thorne's face that he knew very well what was implied.

“In that case you will leave it as it is,” Edith said.

“As far as that goes, you will not likely be there for long. A gentleman of Doctor Thorne's accomplishments will get on quickly in the world if he conducts himself wisely. At Salisbury, a cathedral city, and so close to us, there are better positions going than the living here.”

Dorion's heart speeded, and he looked at Helver with a new interest. “Those positions are largely a matter of patronage,” he said.

“What better patron than a duke?” Helver asked.

"I own to some degree of ambition," Thorne allowed. "I would like to do better for Edith than a small village vicarage, and I believe my own background warrants it."

"And as you mentioned, you won't even be able to set Eddie up a carriage on the small salary that goes with Tisbury."

"I don't mind walking," Edith said at once. "And as far as that goes, Mama would always let us use her carriage. Dorion uses it all the time."

"Still, a better position at Salisbury would allow Dorion to take care of his wife for himself. A man likes to do that, you know, Eddie," Helver informed her.

"Have you a particular position in mind?" Edith asked directly.

"No, but the Dean is getting on. He came to call a few weeks ago — I mentioned it to you, Eddie. I was forcibly struck at his infirmity. It is spoken of that he is close to retirement, is it not, Dorion? His leaving will open up vacancies all down the line."

"I have heard it mentioned," Dorion agreed. "I don't think it likely the post would be offered to me, however."

"Oh, no, but lesser posts will be open, which is what I had in mind," Helver said nonchalantly and sat back to peruse the list of wedding guests, or to pretend he was doing so.

Dorion regarded him suspiciously a long moment, then spoke. "The Duchess *did* mention putting in a word for me."

204

"I shouldn't think Mama has much influence," Helver remarked innocently.

"Not so much as yourself," Thorne said, consideringly.

"Actually, I believe the Bishop appoints the Dean. The Crown, through the Prime Minister, appoints bishops, but the Dean is appointed at the discretion of the Bishop," Helver said.

"The Don of Lazarus College is influential, too, and a good friend of mine," Dorion mentioned. "A man who traffics a good deal in affairs of this nature is the Marquis of Abelmore. It was he who had Jackson made Archdeacon at Salisbury. A word from him would secure the post if I'm not mistaken."

"Ah, yes, Abelmore, a good chap," Helver said. "Quite a friend of my papa's. A pity Papa isn't alive. But you'll make your way without him, Dorion. Keep your eye out for a post in the diocese of Salisbury, and you'll work your way up the ladder in time." Helver was a little surprised to see Thorne's ambitions ran so high. It was clearly the Deanery he was interested in, despite his lack of having performed any lesser offices.

"I am not a young man to waste years in being a vicar of here and a rector of there. My having spent two years at the law before entering the church was a mistake. But it broadens the background. I think my case is rather a special one. It is not every dean who has his doctorate, with a double first."

"That's true," Helver allowed.

"Abelmore is the fellow to approach, all right. I am not personally acquainted with him, however," Dorion said.

"I am not *well* acquainted with him myself."

"But he was a close friend of your father. That will mean something."

"You can't expect Helver to approach him on the matter, Dorion," Edith interrupted. "Really, you have only been Vicar for a few days; it is nonsense to think you have a chance of becoming a dean." Her relief at Dorion's having settled down was routed. He was more ambitious than ever, unreasonably so, and why was Helver egging him on?

Dorion shot a scowl at his fiancée, warning her to silence.

"No, I shouldn't like to do it," Helver agreed.

Dorion's spirits had soared at the mention of becoming a dean. It was a position of prestige and influence and a very good base from which to fly to the Bishop's seat. He longed to kiss the Regent's hand, to live in a palace and be called "His Lordship." To see it all float within his grasp and to float away again for lack of daring and persistence was not to be borne. He looked at his bride, and he looked at the Duke, his two aces, and he figured the most advantageous manner in which to play his hand. Saymore would not do it for himself, but he would do it for Edith — anything within reason, or beyond. If only the simple girl would urge him on; but, no, she sat twiddling a pen between her fingers, not even looking at the Duke.

"Well, Edith, it seems we are not to move to Salisbury," he said. "It will be walking along the dusty roads of Tisbury for you for a while yet."

"I don't mind," she repeated once again.

"We mind it for you, do we not, Your Grace?" Dorion asked.

"Certainly we who care for her would wish to see her better settled. But then you know, Doctor, it removes her from Tisbury, and I shouldn't like that." He looked at Edith and smiled lazily.

She switched her head and applied pen to paper, feeling acutely uncomfortable.

"It is not an impossible distance to travel," Thorne began his urging. "Very close, as you mentioned yourself. Edith would come often to visit her mother, and I hope you would not abandon us entirely yourself."

"I don't think the Dame would like me to come calling on a married daughter," Helver pointed out.

"I am not so jealous," Thorne assured him. "You must always be welcome at the Deanery."

"But would I be welcome by Mrs Thorne?" Helver asked, looking a question at Edith.

She could scarcely believe the tenor of the conversation. She glared at Dorion, waiting for him to express his outrage at Helver's suggestion.

"You and Edith have been friends from childhood. There is no reason friendship need go by the boards on my account," Thorne said.

"I am happy to hear that is *your* view," the Duke said and looked towards Edith. He read the anger in that quarter and continued to Thorne. "It would take a deal of effort to talk Abelmore around. I shouldn't like to think it was all for nothing." He turned back to Edith, looking pointedly at her now, letting his eyes wander over her from head to foot in a manner there was no pretending to misread.

Edith stared at Dorion. He swallowed and sought for a way to deal with his two aces. The Deanery was close enough to taste, and he liked the taste very well. Saymore's reputation was such that neither his intentions nor their seriousness were doubted for a moment. He had always wanted Edith; he was now offering his help to get the position of Dean in return for continued friendship with her. More than friendship — an affair was what he meant, but perhaps some pretence at misunderstanding could be made so as not to turn Saymore off completely.

"Not for nothing, Your Grace. For Edith." This had a blunt sound he rapidly spoke on to overcome. "For an old friend — sister, as you mentioned the other day."

"That is not the relationship I have in mind now," Helver said baldly, taking the thing beyond misunderstanding. He looked levelly at Dorion, as though to impress upon him his meaning. "You understand me?"

"Well, of course she is not your sister. That was only a manner of speaking."

"No, she is not my sister, thank God. About these visits to the Deanery, Thorne, we wouldn't want any scandal to attach to them, because of your position and Edith's — and my own, for that matter."

"Why should scandal attach to them?" Dorion asked, feigning an obtuseness he was far from harbouring.

"Ah, but I mean to visit frequently — at least once a week. I shall miss Eddie very much." His eyes lingered on her, lovingly, covetously.

208

Thorne cleared his throat. "Perhaps Edith should leave us for a moment."

"No, Eddie must stay. I want this perfectly clear between the three of us," Helver said.

"Then by all means let us have it *perfectly clear!*" Edith said, jumping up from her seat. "I can't believe Dorion understands the nature of your bargain, Saymore. He has not had the dubious advantage of your Continental travels."

"Call me Helver, Eddie. Well, Doctor, you understand what I am offering?"

Thorne licked his lips and looked fearfully at Edith. "His Grace is offering to forward my career because of his — affection for you, my dear. As old friends, he is anxious to see you get ahead, and a wife, you know, normally advances her position through her husband. There is nothing wrong in it."

"There is something very wrong when a husband advances his position through his wife's lover. There is a difference *there*, I think you will agree," she pointed out sneeringly.

"Oh, *lover!*" Thorne laughed deprecatingly. "*Friend* is the word we are using, and in this case it is the wife who has the influential friends."

"Use whatever euphemism suits you, Thorne," Helver said, "but pray confine yourself to the single. I already dislike very much the notion of sharing her with you. You mustn't be playing other cards behind my back. There are to be no other lovers."

"I am not being *shared* by anyone!" Edith shouted, her bosom heaving.

"It is only a manner of speaking, my dear," Thorne said, trying to calm her. Damme, why did Saymore have to put it into so many words right in front of her? He would have expected more *finesse* from him. "His Grace does not wish to lose your company. He means to call on us, that's all." Thorne darted a look of warning, of pleading, at Helver, who ignored it entirely.

"That's all, Eddie. Just discreet calls in the afternoon or evening when the Doctor is busy elsewhere, but no one need know that. I explained to you, you recall, how it is done in Italy. And really, you know, you said I might be your *cavaliere servente* after you were married."

"Dorion!" Edith said to her groom in a strangled voice.

He cleared his throat and then laughed. "What foolish notions are you getting in your head, my love? You know His Grace better than I. You must know his intentions are not harmful to you." He cast one last appealing glance at Helver for help.

"I wouldn't hurt a hair of her head," he said lovingly. "The last thing in the world I would ever do is hurt Eddie. I love her too much for that, and, if she dislikes it, the arrangement is not to be thought of."

"But what *is* the arrangement?" she asked, in some confusion. She found it hard to believe still that she had it right. Dorion would not take it so calmly if it were as she thought.

In his worst nightmares, Thorne had not thought to see the matter come to a head in this awful way. That Edith and Helver were mutually attracted, he knew, and

210

saw a clandestine romance developing between them while he obligingly remained unaware. That it should be put into black and white before the marriage, and in front of the bride, was a folly beyond imagining.

"The explanation had best come from your groom-to-be," Helver said, looking at Thorne expectantly.

"I'm afraid I don't understand," he said.

"I thought I had made myself clear," Helver replied calmly. "I want Edith. I will do my best to advance you — though I can't promise the Dean's position so soon — in exchange for her." There — the cards were on the table, and it was all or nothing. He looked at Thorne, and he looked at Eddie, who stared at him as though he were a dragon. For an instant his resolve wavered. He read the indecision in Thorne's eyes and feared he was about to turn holy on him, become a pillar of outraged virtue. "Well?" he asked.

"It's up to Edith," Thorne answered, washing his hands of the affair, like Pontius Pilate.

"Leave us," Helver said to Thorne, but his eyes were fixed on Edith, trying to convey some message she was too distraught to read.

"Edith hasn't answered," he objected.

"Leave us," Helver repeated without raising his voice. In fact, he lowered it somewhat, but still it held an air of authority.

Thorne clenched his fists — looked at them both — then crept out on his shuffling feet, to pace the hall and fret and hope that Edith wouldn't botch the scheme. It was unforgivable of Saymore to have put it straight before her in such a fashion. One would have thought a man of the world would manage his amours more discreetly. He would never forgive him for that.

Helver watched him leave, then turned to Edith with a mocking smile on his face. "What do you think of your holy man now?" he asked.

In that flashing instant she hated Saymore. Any last trace of the boy was gone. Here was a man she didn't know — cruel, mocking, degenerate. "You're beastly!" she said, her face white, with two dark, glowing eyes staring at him in revolted fascination.

"Eddie!" he leapt up, surprised. "You can't think I meant it! You know me better than that."

"You meant it. I think you had best leave, Your Grace."

"Don't call me that! I'm not a stranger!"

"You are. I don't know you, or want to. I've never known you. You're *evil*. Mama and all the rest of them were right, and I was wrong. I tried not to see what you were — tried to fool myself you weren't as bad as you are — that you'd grow up one day, change. Well, you have. You're a full-grown, hardened rake now. Or worse, if there is anything worse."

"There's something worse all right! There's that damned creeping hypocrite, spouting morality — a churchman willing to sell his wife for a promotion. I may be bad, but I'd never do that. I've never bought or sold a woman yet."

"No, you've just taken what you wanted and cast it aside when you were through with it. Lady De Courcy and Bessie Moog and all the others."

"I didn't!"

212

"And didn't play the *cavaliere servente* in Italy, either, I imagine. Didn't seduce Widow Malone when you were still a boy."

"She was the one did the seducing, an old woman and I was only sixteen."

"You bought her with a cheap set of garnets, and you bought Bessie Moog with a new house, so don't bother telling me you never bought a woman."

"I never intended to buy *you*. I had no intention of making him a dean."

"A welcher into the bargain!"

"Eddie, it wasn't *that*!" he said desperately.

"Liar! Liar — hypocrite — rake! Go away!" she shouted.

He took a step towards her and could see she was deadly earnest, even trembling with it. It had all happened before. They were in the meadow with Larry, and she preferred Larry. She wouldn't believe him, and in frustration he raised his hand and struck her across the cheek. Her head was jerked to the side with the force of it. She looked at him in bewildered disbelief, her mouth open.

Helver looked at her, and then at his open hand, horrified to see what he had done. A strangled, incoherent sound came from his throat, and he reached out his arms towards her.

Her face crumpled and tears spurted into her eyes. To his astonishment, she sobbed and said, "I'm sorry, Helver," and pitched herself into his arms.

"Eddie — don't! Don't say that!" he whispered in an unsteady voice and crushed her head against his chest.

"I'm sorry, darling. Oh, God! I'm sorry, Eddie. I didn't mean to do it. Truly, I didn't. I lost my head. I — oh, don't you hate me, too. I couldn't bear it. I don't mind the others. Don't *you* hate me, Eddie."

"I don't hate you, Helver," she sniffed in a small voice.

"You should. It's all true. I am rotten, but I didn't mean what I said to Thorne. I had to show you what he is. He'd have sold you, Eddie. He doesn't love you a bit."

"I know. I don't care about him. I know you didn't mean it."

"I didn't, I swear. And I didn't mean to hit you. If I ever strike you again I'll cut off my arm. Forgive me, Eddie. I'll never do it again."

"It's all right." She rubbed at her wet eyes with her knuckles and tried to draw away from him, but he pulled her back and held her tightly.

"It's not all right. It was a terrible thing to do," he said fiercely. "Don't heap coals on my head by saying it's all right. Hit me — beat me — do anything, but don't hate me. I need you, Eddie. I couldn't bear it without you."

"Bear what?" she asked, ever blunt.

"Everything — life, work, the Hall, the village, the whole world. When I thought you were going to marry him I was driven mad. I must have been crazy to . . . you didn't love him, did you?"

"No, I hated him."

"Why were you marrying him, then?"

214

"Because — because he asked me, and Mama accepted, and there wasn't anyone else. There wasn't any pack of suitors, Helver. I lied, too, to try to make you jealous."

"You didn't have to try. I've been so jealous for a week I nearly burst. I've been fighting with Forringer and Mama and even snapped at Travers a couple of times. What will the Dame say?"

"I don't care what she says. I'm not marrying Dorion."

"You're marrying me, of course," he said simply.

"Why didn't you ask me sooner?"

"By the time I found out how much I loved you, you were engaged. Have you cared for me all along, ever since I've been back?"

"For years. Ages before you left."

"You hid it very well. Never a word or a sign to me. Or was I just too blind to see it?" He looked long at her, and he could see it now, shining in her eyes. "I've never kissed you — in all the years we've been friends. We're engaged now. It's all right?" With this unwonted propriety he kissed her lightly on the cheek, still red from his hand.

"It will be one of those grand passions, won't it? Like Dante and Beatrice, only we'll be married?" she asked, smiling at him.

"Better than Dante and Beatrice. A Divine Passion," he promised. And when at last he really kissed her, she saw that Helver was right, as usual. It was some elemental force beyond resisting or wanting to.

Cradling her face between his hands he regarded her closely. "You do believe me, don't you, that what I said to Thorne was only a trick? I could hardly go through with it when I saw you were taking me seriously. What must you have thought of me?"

"Oh, I thought it wouldn't be quite as dull as I feared, being Mrs Thorne," she said impishly.

"Have I ruined your character at a touch?"

"You ruined it years ago, feeding me wine and making me sniff brandy. I'm well prepared to be your wife now."

"I think I was preparing you for it all along without realizing it. But really, I'm not as bad as Thorne."

"I can't quite believe he understood you."

"He understood, all right. He isn't the saint you've believed. But now that he's not marrying you, I don't hate him so much as I did. He might never have agreed to what I suggested if I hadn't put the notion in his head and lured him along with the Dean's chair. How the gudgeon thought I could get it for him is beyond me."

"If he thought it, you may be sure he's right. He knows all the tricks and angles for getting ahead. But I never thought he'd be so low as to use *me* as one of his tools."

"He'd use his own mother — but never mind him. Eddie, we're going to be happy together. Coming so close to losing you has taught me a lesson. I'm through with gallivanting and flirting. I *have* changed. I've been wanting to settle down to a more regular life, and it was never anyone but you I wanted to settle down with. Mr

216

and Mrs Smith, only we'll live at the Hall instead of one of the little cottages."

"And I *will* have an upholstered settee, and a maid to bring me a glass of wine. And I'll have the Duchess and Aunt Sara and Uncle Egbert, too," she added less enthusiastically.

"Devil a bit of it. Travers will convince them they'll be more comfortable at the Dower House. I never did get the roof fixed, and they've been threatening to move out for a month. We'll fill all the rooms up with children as fast as we can, to keep them out."

"You have over thirty bedrooms, Helver."

"Thirty-five, but we'll give each of them a suite and a room for their nannies. Say an even dozen. I didn't like being an only child."

"Neither did I, but I don't know that I'd have liked eleven brothers and sisters."

"We'll start with one and see how we take to being parents. I mean to get the boys' noses to the grindstone as soon as they're breached and keep it there. It was a mistake on my father's part, I think, to give me so much free time. And you will be in charge of the girls. I don't want them roaming the meadows — God only knows what heathens they'll fall in with."

Their foolish love-making was interrupted by a tap at the door, and Thorne looked in. His eyebrows rose an inch to see his bride encircled in the Duke of Saymore's arms. "What is going on?" he asked sharply.

"I'm taking over your wife a little prematurely," Helver said with a mocking smile. "In fact, we've decided you are expendable, Doctor. Eddie don't like triangles. She never cared for geometry in the least."

"Edith, I must ask . . ." he began, but was interrupted.

"I would prefer if you call my wife Miss Durden till it is proper to call her Duchess," Helver said. "But, really, I think it best if you not call her anything at all. Any questions you have to ask in regard to this matter, you will please direct to me. And before you pester me with a dozen, I shall outline the position. You are not marrying Miss Durden; you are not to be Vicar at Tisbury. In fact, you are not to show your damned creeping form within the bounds of my village."

"I have a contract!"

"For a year. I will be happy to forfeit the three hundred pounds without availing myself of your services. I shall seek a moral mentor elsewhere, Doctor. I don't care for the brand of morality you perpetrate, nor does Miss Durden. Three hundred should enable you to get beyond my grasp. If you are wise, you will do so."

"Dame Durden . . ."

"Yes, she adores your Saxon blood but won't care for that Italian streak of Machiavelli, if it becomes necessary for her to hear of it. You're exposed, Thorne, and you'd better get farther away than Bath, for you're through there, too. In fact, if you will take a piece of advice from your ex-student, you will do well to revert to your initial studies of the law. Scandal has a way of getting around, and the stench you're picking up won't serve you so well in the church as in the law — or

218

politics. Really, you would make an admirable politician. I believe you have an innate ability for double-dealing that will see you Prime Minister before ten years are out."

"This was all your idea!"

"It was, and I accept full responsibility for it. As my spiritual guide, however, you ought to have hinted me to a more proper course instead of encouraging me at every opportunity to covet your bride. It is a poor guide who is led astray by his pupil."

"I had no intention of allowing you and Edith to . . ."

"You had no intention of trying to stop me. Cut line, Thorne. The jig's up. If you are at all wise you will leave before the necessary explanations are made to Dame Durden. I am only trying to save you from additional embarrassment, but my heart isn't quite in it."

"You haven't heard the end of this!"

"Better for you if I have," Helver said with a laugh. "The *other* end, you know, involves the Court of Twelve Paces; and in my flaming career that is one court I have managed to stay out of. But I feel I can acquit myself well enough if it comes to that."

For a moment Thorne wanted to walk forward and strike the Duke of Saymore's taunting face. He took one pace — even a firm one, with his heel striking the floor — then his inborn sense of self-preservation took over, and he turned and crept from the room. Helver and Edith were still together talking when the front door slammed, and they saw him leave.

Looking at his back through the window, Edith said, "He'll have to walk all the way to the village."

"Not he! He'll be picked up by some gig before he's gone half a mile. His sort always makes out in the world."

CHAPTER
SEVENTEEN

Thorne had been gone for half an hour and, though the lovers didn't know it, was comfortably ensconced in the carriage — not gig — of Squire Rigby on his comfortable way to London. His mind seethed with plans. His three hundred he would get by applying to the Bank in Tisbury, he decided, to avoid direct contact with Saymore. It didn't do to have dealings with such disreputable characters as that one. It would be known before long that his moral scruples had revolted at being Vicar to such a blackguard. A close questioning of Squire Rigby gave him Lady De Courcy's address in the metropolis, and he passed the trip pleasantly by selecting an address for himself within walking distance of her without cutting too seriously into his three hundred. A trip to Lazarus College to see the Don would also be necessary to see what livings were vacant.

The time was also passing pleasantly at the Court. "The Dame won't like it," Helver remarked to his bride. "Shall I tell her, or would it come best from you?"

"We'll both tell her before you leave. But whatever she says, Helver, it won't make any difference. She is a worse judge of character than I am myself, and I won't be talked out of it by her."

"I personally am prepared to dash to the border if necessary. The village will expect no better of me, though I would prefer to do it up in style for your sake."

"If Mama objects, we could be married from the Hall. Or will your Mama object, too?"

"She never objects to anything but the roof, and Sara and Egbert like you. They will all be amazed at your having me."

They hadn't much longer to wait to discover the Dame's attitude. She soon came into the living room and stopped a yard inside the door to behold the sight before her eyes. Edith sat very close to Helver on the sofa, their hands intertwined, their heads together. It looked so right, so natural to see them there — as if little Helver were again her playmate — that the Dame's eyes actually moistened up. But sense soon returned.

"Edith!" she said in alarm. "Where's Dorion? What are you thinking of, child?" Yet even as she spoke she noticed the glow of happiness on her daughter's face. Such a different face than she had been wearing since her engagement to Thorne. Helver was looking at her, too, with such a tender expression — such love — that she had grave misgivings as to what she had wrought in forcing the wedding of her own choice.

"He's gone, Mama," Edith said, edging away from Helver and extracting her hand from his.

222

"Gone where? What has been going on in my absence?"

"I have been making advances to your daughter," Helver said fairly firmly. "I know you don't favour my suit, Dame Durden, but I am pressing it forward all the same."

"Oh, Helver!" the Dame fretted. "It's too late. Why didn't you come forward in the proper way when you got home if you wanted to marry Edith?"

"Because I didn't think you'd let me in, and besides, I didn't know I wanted to marry Eddie till it was too late. But I do want to, and she's turned Thorne off; so I mean to badger and pester you till you give your consent." His voice became firmer as he spoke, seeing that she didn't flare up at him.

"Turned Thorne off? Why?" She tried to sound angry but some soaring in her heart prevented it, and there was even a half smile trying to find a place on her lips. "Oh, dear, what must he think? I don't know why you always have to do things in such a scrambling, uncivilized way, Helver. We shall have to face him every Sunday, and I for one blush to see him again."

Helver was amazed at the lightness of the attack. Not a word about forbidding the match, and a full-blown smile now quite open on the Dame's usually worried face. "You won't have to see him. He isn't to be our new Vicar. Under the circumstances . . ."

"I hope it was his idea; you surely didn't sack him, as well as steal his bride!"

"Not exactly."

"Helver was very generous, Mama. He gave him a year's salary," Edith said.

"Did you indeed, Helver? Well, that was very generous of you. But you were never clutch-fisted. No one ever said that of you."

She walked towards the sofa but sat in a chair instead, as intrusion on the two seemed inappropriate.

"Have I your consent, Dame Durden, to court Edith?" he asked.

"Consent? Much difference it would make if I forbade it! You'd be sneaking off to meadows. Well, you have my consent, but mind you come to the door like a gentleman, Helver. I won't have the neighbours talking about Edith as if she were just one of your flirts."

"It would be best to make a formal announcement. We'll do it today, and that way the villagers will have a legitimate piece of news to discuss. And, Dame Durden, we don't want to wait awfully long to get married."

"No, the sooner the better. Well, we have a wedding half planned, so that is no problem." She did feel, though, that with bringing a mongrel into the family, and titled mongrel blood at that, stewed goldfinches and boars' heads might be out of place. "I'll discuss it with your mother," she decreed, her spine stiffening.

"Shall I ask her to call on you?" Helver asked, well aware that this last statement indicated an unprecedented change in the Dame's normal behaviour. He wished to put forward the option that would be less galling to the Dame, but as no calls between the two homes had ever been made, he didn't know which to mention.

"I'll call at the Hall," the Dame said. It was to be complete capitulation.

"That's very kind of you, Ma'am," Helver said and looked his amazement at his bride.

"Edith has been to call, and, if we are to be connected with this marriage, I must make the best of it. I daresay you'll be wanting champagne and lobster patties and that sort of fare for your wedding feast." Tudor times were being tossed to the winds, and a new era was settling in at Durden Court.

"And a smoked boar's head with rosemary leaves," Helver added, smiling. "Don't change for us, Dame Durden."

"Edith will be changing, and I don't mean to lose her," she answered simply.

Edith ran to her mother and threw her arms around her. "I'm not changing, Mama. Helver knows me exactly as I am and wants to marry Dame Durden's daughter."

"I always thought you had a good head on your shoulders, despite your pranks," she allowed through a mist of tears. When Helver heard his scarlet past become a series of pranks, he felt much better about himself.

"I always came closer to beating the quintain than any of them," he reminded her. "Yes, and I *will* beat it next year."

"You only want to get to kiss the Queen of the May," Edith jeered.

"Only if the Queen of the May is you," he answered readily.

"We don't bother with that any more," the Dame said.

"I wish you hadn't given it up. Couldn't we have it, just once more?" Helver asked.

The Dame looked at him with quickening interest. "I suppose we *could* . . . But mid-summer's eve is closer. In the old days it was the custom to have bonfires . . ."

"I love bonfires," Helver said, both to appease her and because he did like any sort of pleasant nonsense.

Her thoughts ran to white garlands for the lintels, and at the back of her mind she remembered she had a dozen goldfinches she had been trapping for Edith and Dorion's wedding feast.

She wrote up the announcement herself, not noticing that her pen flew over the page, whereas it had dragged along when accepting Thorne's offer. At the corner of her lips a smile hovered. Durden Court would remain Tudorish during her own lifetime; but she would go often to the Hall, and there she would enter the nineteenth century. The Tudors had actually been forward-looking people, she recalled. Especially the last of them, Elizabeth I, with her sending her sailors out to conquer new worlds.

It was a month till the wedding, during which time she vacillated between being more Tudorish than the Tudors and giving way to the sweeping wind of change that followed hard at Helver Trebourne's heels. He was still Helver Trebourne to her and not the Duke, though Edith was already mentally assigned the title of Duchess.

226

In the village the news was a boon. It was said that Dame Durden, for all her talk of Saxon blood, had been happy enough to exchange it for good old blue mongrel blood when it was all said and done, and likely it was the Duke she had had in her eye all the while, with her airs and graces. There was plenty to talk of that month. The wedding, the loss of their Vicar under *such strange* circumstances, and soon his replacement, a single gentleman from Devonshire with a tidy property of his own there, they heard. He had to have a wife chosen for him. The house across from the apothecary shop was sold to a retired merchant from London, rich, they soon learned, and with two daughters and a son that gave themselves fine discussable airs. Helver Trebourne was not doing much to amuse them, but then the lad had to grow up sometime.

They occasionally forgot his past and accidentally called him the Duke, but to his bride he was still Helver, the beloved friend of her childhood grown up. And sometimes not too grown up either.

"Shall we leave this mess and move into one of the cottages?" he asked her when he took her to inspect her new home, whose second storey was damp and becoming mildewed.

The sound of hammers on the roof came to them quite forcibly. "What — three bedrooms, and us with a dozen children to house? Goodness, I don't blame your relatives for moving to the Dower House, but I wish Travers had stayed with us."

"We'll lure her back when we get the nursery started. Try if you can keep her out! But she was always as discreet as a diplomat. She knows we'll want to be alone at first."

"I like Travers. I don't mind if she's here."

"I do," he said, drawing her into his arms. "We couldn't do this if she were always with us." He kissed her lightly on the lips.

"She wouldn't *always* be with us. Just sometimes."

"That means that sometimes I couldn't kiss you, and I want to. All the time."

"Do you, Helver?" she asked, well satisfied with his limited ambition.

"No, sometimes I want to do a great deal more," he warned with a charming smile.

When Travers slipped quietly past the door, returned to the Hall purposely to have a word with Edith, she thought it discreet not to intrude. Helver was doing what he always wanted to do and nothing more, but he was doing it with such enthusiasm that it seemed a shame to interrupt him.